How We Became Fat

A Novel

PRAKASH SESHADRI

Prakash Seshadri Wilmington 2015

Printed in the United States of America

First Printing, 2015
ISBN-13: 9780996319317
ISBN-10: 099631931X
www.howwebecamefat.com
https://www.facebook.com/howwebecamefat
This is a work of fiction. Names, characters, businesses, places, events and incidents are either the products of the author's imagination or used in a fictitious manner. Any resemblance to actual persons, living or dead, or actual events is purely coincidental.

This book is not intended as a substitute for the medical advice of physicians. The reader should regularly consult a physician in matters relating to his/her health and particularly with respect to any symptoms that may require diagnosis or medical attention.

To my wife for all her support

Chapter 1

"My sweet little William."

Willie Barnes was sitting in the pool hall drinking his usual Jack Daniel's and Dr. Pepper. He swirled his glass around until the amber liquid inside nearly came out. It was early and the scent of cigarettes and hard working men's body odor did not cloud the air until mid-afternoon. Willie had on a flattened hat that was grey and purple. He wore a saddle brown, super-soft leather jacket. The collars were wide and the whole jacket gave him an hourglass figure. He was five-foot-ten inches tall, thin, with wide shoulders, a skinny waist, and flared hips. His glass reflected off his dark sunglasses with gold rims. The whisky traveled past his full stubble beard.

"Hey Neptune, isn't it early for you to be drinking so hard?" a man muttered from behind the bar. He was in his mid-fifties and his head was completely shaved. He was cleaning glasses with a rag and facing a black-and-white television hanging on the wall. He turned around and snatched Willie's empty glass.

"I've clocked off. You know I do shift work and this is my evening off. I give you the same old answers every day. Why quiz me? You should be glad that someone actually comes into this place, especially with the grand décor. Fred, what do you call the style? Dumpese?" Willie needled with a smile on his face.

The bartender looked puzzled. His right eyebrow rose, "What are you talking about? Dumpese? What is dumpese? You kids are always making up names. Dumpese?"

"Yeah, you've got Chinese, Japanese, and this place is Dumpese. Webster's would define it, 'Dumpese: from the culture of dump'." Willie smirked. He hated being questioned about his business. Who did Fred think he was? His sarcasm was part fun and part an expression of disdain for inner-city Washington. These old-timers thought they were all mentors because they were the only old black men in the neighborhood. The senior men had businesses, mostly intact nuclear families and continued to live in the old neighborhood. Willie believed that particularly Fred and his old bar had taken part in breaking up some of the families in the neighborhood.

Fred picked up a wooden bat from underneath the bar counter. His eyes widened and he looked like he was going to take out some generational rage. To Fred, this corrupt, lazy generation had reduced his neighborhood to brick rubble so that his joint was now the sole building standing. "I will Dumpese your head if you like. Now you are always saying you are doing shift work. I know you. You are too soft to be working in the loading docks or driving trucks around here."

"Soft? I've got five that will give you a good face massage if you want to find out how tough I am," Willie raised his fist to Fred and finished his whisky. This was play fighting despite their subtle animosities. He was only goofing around with Fred, whose bar was next to his parents' old store. Willie wanted the questioning to end, and wanted his life to be different but he also realized it was important to keep life light in the 'hood. The 1970s was, after all, an era that was full of depression and darkness.

"Boy, you're ridiculous. I think I know what you do, which is just like all the other boys in this place." Fred frowned. If you didn't work at the docks, or the hotels, or do nothing, a young man in this neighborhood sold drugs. Today, Fred appeared ready to draw blood and reclaim the neighborhood for the good old times.

"And what would that be, old man?" Willie took a more angry tone. He didn't like the lazy stereotype given to his generation. The older folks planted the seeds and the apple did not fall far from the tree. He wondered who he could impress. It was bad enough that he felt the scorn of whites as a whole. He was an alien on his own planet.

"Do you really think I am that naive? You walk around with those gold chains and that fancy coat like you're a player. You've got that fancy Lincoln parked in front of my place. What do I think you are? Let me see … An AM kindergarten teacher. You get here right when the kids get out. I see, it's stressful," Fred said cynically. He wanted a straight answer from the young man. He loved the old neighborhood. He saw in Willie a microcosm of the degradation of the entire neighborhood. Fred continued, "Of course I know what you do. You're a fancy smack dealer, just like all the other hoodlums here. You even have some fancy degree from that college in Baltimore—a white boys' school—so I don't get why you need to be coming back to the neighborhood for this shit. I see it. Because you're so well dressed and I get all these stupid phone calls here for you from Capitol Hill, you must be dealin' to those slimy politicians. It's like you're getting taken twice or more than that. I said my piece for today." He didn't want politicians to denigrate his neighborhood, and good souls such as Willie's parents should beget good people.

Willie dropped his head from the black and white images of the World Series on the TV and nodded. He was very angry at the assumption that he was a dealer. "You know my history. I had a cousin who was hooked and OD'd. Why the hell would I want to do that? I want to get ahead but I'm not going to mess with drugs. I've got to take care of things. If you don't need my business, I can always drink somewhere else. But I think I'll keep coming here just to make you mad. It's a free country. Besides you've got real dealers coming here later in the evening. Hold your fire for them. Let me have another." Willie picked up the empty glass and pointed the open end toward Fred.

This had been an ongoing conversation for both of them since he had started his new job. Willie needed a contact spot that wasn't his home. The drink soothed him and he liked the proximity to his parents' old store, which brought him positive memories. He sat there waiting for Fred to get him a refill.

The phone behind the bar went off. Fred walked close to the tiered bottles to answer it, "Rock Bottom's, what'd you need?" Fred poured the whisky into

Willie's glass with the phone headset balanced between his shoulder and his ear and opened a can of Dr. Pepper to mix into it. "Yeah, he's here. Could you make an appointed time before he gets here and then meet him later. This is a proper establishment. I am not Willie's secretary." Fred took his ear off the phone and dragged it to the place at the bar where Willie was sitting. "Your customers are waiting." Fred pointed the black receiver between Willie's eyes.

Willie took it and spoke into the phone. "I can meet you there," he replied. "Yeah, I know Dan's. I can meet you there. There's a pit stop I need to make first." Willie handed the receiver to Fred. "Thanks, Moneypenny." Willie stood up and left a couple of bills on the table. He had to run errands and had no time for Fred's taunting.

Fred followed him to the door. "*007* my ass. Don't be stupid, your folks wouldn't want that," Fred barked as the door closed behind Willie.

✳   ✳   ✳

Willie walked out to the curb where his light metallic-green Lincoln Continental was parked. Willie walked to the driver side with his hand on the white vinyl roof and looked at the lot next to Rock Bottom's with a blank stare. He remembered the smell of burnt ashes from his youth when his parents' flower shop had been freshly razed to the ground. Their store had been gone for many years but the freshness of the burning always seemed to come to him when leaving Fred's bar. The tragedy reminded him that before it he'd led a different, ideal life and maybe, on a different timeline, a fortunate Willie was living a better present.

He made a stop at a local pharmacy. A homeless man sat with his back leaning on a wall next to the entrance. The man faced the street with a glassy stare and held an empty cup out. The man didn't ask for anything. Willie quickly walked into the pharmacy to avoid the stench of urine coming from the man. Hunchbacked women in their mid-seventies droned through the aisles pushing their walkers and staring at all the infirmity-lessening goods on the shelves. He walked past this plodding obstacle course and made it to the pharmacy counter. A forty-year-old Jamaican woman approached the register and looked at Willie.

"Pickup for Edna Stevens. Here you go," she said with her island accent and handed the small paper bag to him. "How have you been, handsome?" she asked boldly.

"Thanks," Willie answered curtly and took the bag. He recalled she had only been in the United States for five years and had just begun working there a few months ago. She was single and paid Willie a lot of attention. Willie thought she was a beautiful woman for her age but he was not interested in a woman who was fifteen years his senior. He smiled back and thanked her. Willie reversed his course past the hunchbacked ladies and passed a young girl dragging a two-year-old by her side. "Hey Laticia, how are things?" Willie asked politely.

"Good, Willie, good." Laticia bobbed her head underneath the faux fur rimmed hood of her black coat. A bright eyed child was tugging her arm toward the shelves of candy bars below the front register. The pom pom of his hat bobbed up and down as he tried to extricate himself from his mother's grasp.

Willie knew that this sixteen-year-old girl had been his twenty-three-year-old cousin Ellington's girlfriend two years ago. That was approximately the age of the little boy by her side. It was shortly after his birth that his cousin died of an overdose. Whether his overdose was an exuberant celebration of his birth, agony about his ability to care for a child, or just plain addiction, no one understood why his cousin had taken so much. He never knew what Laticia saw in him. El had been hooked on drugs since he was thirteen. Willie believed their relationship was the time-honored tradition of a girl falling for a rebel or a lost boy. Willie smiled and left her there standing awkwardly. He had nothing in common with her except for his dead cousin. She followed him with her eyes as he approached his car, waiting for a look back from him, a connection.

Willie jumped back in his Lincoln. The door scraped the high curb when he got in and he cursed himself at the thought of the chipped paint. On his way home, he drove by many abandoned cars. The neighborhood took on the quality of a prison in the fall. The brick and cement houses and grey streets formed the walls and floor. Greenery meant freedom from a grey cement cage. To Willie, the liberation was exponential to the lusciousness of the neighborhood. As he drove around, the air coming in through the crack in his car window was sterile. There was no smell of decaying leaves as he remembered from the wooded campus of his college days.

Willie parked his car, and got out, being careful not to scratch the door again. When he was about twenty feet from his destination, he heard the creaking. The rhythmic crackling of wood on wood got louder as he climbed the steps. He noticed her swollen ankles bursting from her black shoes. He saw them rocking back and forth with his first step, the rest of her hidden by the stairwell and porch post. With the next step, he saw her white compression stockings meet the end of her skirt, and finally, when he was past the post at the top of the balcony, he saw her smiling face.

"My sweet little William," the woman in the chair cooed through her missing front teeth. Edna was in her mid-sixties but looked older. Her grey hair was parted in the middle and curled toward her face just below her ears. Fluid had collected in her legs because of a weakened heart. Her physique was otherwise of a fairly thin woman, accentuated by sunken cheeks. She was not ashamed of the edema and wore a blue flower print skirt that showed her edematous ankles. Her arms opened wide as Willie approached.

"I've got your diabetes medication," Willie said and put the little white wax bag next to his grandmother on the table, kissed her on the cheek, and crouched down to hug her. He ran errands for his grandmother on a regular basis. Almost every other week, he would go to the pharmacy for her. She took over twenty tablets that always seemed to need refilling at different times of the month. The tablets also seemed to change every time she saw a new specialist.

Edna usually sat here and rocked the day away until it got well below freezing. The people-watching and idle conversation with her neighbors filled her days. She had lived in that house for nearly thirty years. She watched her neighbors go to work, go to war, get evicted, and get high. It was ever-dynamic, but no match for the presence of William, who reminded her of his mother, Dorothy. Dorothy was the only one of her children who had stayed close; the rest had scattered around the country. She thought she had given all of them a good home they would want to come back to, but she found that their dispersal was the result of a Washington home not able to provide them sustenance.

Willie looked at the framed picture on a wicker side table next to Edna's rocking chair. It was a black and white picture of a proud husband in a suit and a demure smiling wife standing in front of their newly purchased flower shop. Willie lived there until he was thirteen. Despite the fact that unemployment was climbing and businesses were closing, Willie's parents made a good living. Unfortunately, there was still good money in selling flowers to funeral homes. He noticed the sign next to the store: "Ro…Bo…" The rest of Fred the bartender's sign had been cut off by the wooden picture frame. He also noticed the singed edges of the picture. The picture brought back memories of that horrible night. He remembered the smell of ashes again and felt his body getting hot.

It was just like the hell described by the pastor of his family church. The fire had started at the back of the store and crept up the back wall. Willie lived right above the florist sign, his parents on the other side. As soon as Willie smelled smoke, he turned the scalding brass knob and flung open the door. A crimson and yellow curtain greeted him and formed a wall to his parents' room but the stairs were clear. He yelled repeatedly to his parents but ran quickly down the stairs, driven by self-preservation. He stood barefoot in his pajamas by Fred and his patrons and watched the conflagration. The store burned until there was only a brick skeleton left with his parents inside. Willie later learned that the store next to his parents on the opposite side of Rock Bottom's was abandoned. His parents apparently died as a result of a botched attempt at insurance fraud. Like in all tragedies, the questions rose within him, "why?" or "why not me?"

Willie broke his daze and remembered his appointment. "I've gotta go," he told his grandmother.

Edna frowned with disappointment and slowly looked down at her hands. She resumed rocking at a creeping pace. "Alright then," she sighed softly, as if it was another one of her children leaving her for good.

Willie felt a lump in his throat as the guilt rolled over him. He looked at his Rolex watch. "Oh, I think I have some time."

Edna's head lifted and she smiled. Willie sat down for some sweet tea and toast with his grandmother. The meeting at Dan's could wait a few more minutes.

Chapter 2

"It is in the best interest of food companies to make their foods saltier and sweeter, so that we keep coming back for more."

The lights dimmed on the Syracuse Health Science Center's auditorium. The third lecture in a series on disease prevention by the medical school's community health forum was about to begin. The featured speaker was Charles S. Mohr, MD, a noted obesity specialist. Dr. Mohr's silhouette was diametrically opposite to most of his patients, at least prior to therapy. He stood six feet two inches tall and had a thin, lanky appearance. He nearly never needed to shave his acne-marked face. The pocks and scars gave him ruggedness and his high cheek bones gave presence. From afar, one thought he looked like Abraham Lincoln sans the stovepipe hat. He wore a grey suit with a white shirt and an equally bland tie that blended perfectly into the wall behind him.

Dr. Mohr was giving the lecture he usually gave to lay people—what physicians on any lecture circuit called a boxed talk—about the definition and causes of obesity and what individuals and the community could do about it. Like much of America, upstate New York had seen a recent surge in obesity. For Dr. Mohr, it was a simple lecture that gave communities an understanding of weight issues and also netted him a decent speaker's fee.

While Dr. Mohr gave lectures all the time he was always terrified until he began to speak. Although he resembled Lincoln, he did not have the heroic president's confidence as an orator. The hair touching his collar on the back of head always stood on end, but he knew if he started his lecture out right, he could build his confidence and get through it without stammering. *What do I have to prove? It's not like I am trying to get a National Institutes of Health grant,* he told himself which calmed him a bit and lowered his heart rate. For a grant application, a panel of experts would take apart any theory thrown in front of them to discern quality science. He had been in that brain-teaser 'lion's den' only once and had his dreams of academic research flushed. An attentive ear was all he sought at this venue. All he had to do was reset the context of the talk so it fit the audience he was presenting it to. The relative lack of knowledge of the lay community members and few scattered internists gave him even more confidence. Still, sweat was beading on his brow, puddles of sweat hid under his grey jacket and his heart palpated as if anticipating the start of the 'big game.' He wrung his hands and dabbed his forehead with a handkerchief from his suit pocket. He did not notice the fresh lipstick stain on it and fortunately it did not smear his skin. It was lucky he hadn't seen it anyway, for it would have thrown his speech off kilter.

The dean of the medical school stood up at the dais and Dr. Mohr heard parts of his introduction: "A graduate of New York Medical College…residency at Georgetown Medical Center…current director of the Eastern Shore Weight Management Clinic…Dr…"

Dr. Mohr walked up to the podium, stumbling on a microphone wire. The lights were bright, nearly blinding him, but that was okay. As long as he couldn't see anyone's eyes looking at him, there was no one out there to hear his lecture. The auditorium held one hundred and eighty people, but the intense light made them a comforting blur. His racing heart slowed to a reasonable gallop. He disliked giving lectures in small rooms where he could feel the soul-piercing eyes of the audience; talks where he felt as if the audiences' lashes rubbed his skin when they blinked. It was the distance in a vast auditorium that gave him the impression that he was lecturing on the moon and it lessened his stage fright.

He began by telling the crowd the definition of obesity: "Obesity, according to the World Health Organization, is defined by an index called the Body Mass Index, or BMI. This is the measurement of one's weight in kilograms divided by one's height in meters squared, an approximation of the human body's surface area." The slide behind Dr. Mohr showed an Alfred Hitchcock-like outline of an obese man next to the picture of a table with the various classifications of obesity. The body mass index placed people in cutoff categories of obese, over-weight and normal. He went on to explain that a body mass index of greater than thirty was defined as obese. He emphasized to the audience that the cutoff didn't mean a person with a body mass index of twenty nine and classified as overweight, not obese, was in the clear. It was a continuum of risk in which the higher a person's BMI the greater their risk of heart disease and diabetes.

"So I have provided all of you with a chart that has done the BMI calculations for you. I want you all to look at the top of the chart - that is the weight. I want you to find your weight."

The people in the audience picked up the sheets of paper with the colored BMI table. Some squinted at the sheets because despite the brightness shone on Dr. Mohr, the audience seating area was relatively dark.

"Now I want you to look on the left side of the table and follow down from the weight to your height. That is your current body mass index."

The crowd began a unified mumble. A few people in the audience started laughing as others scoffed in disbelief.

"I am not going to ask you to share this with everyone in the audience," Dr. Mohr reassured them, "but I also do not want you to feel alone if you're surprised at what you've found. About twenty-five percent of all Americans are obese." Dr. Mohr proceeded to show the crowd slides of the continental United States and the gradual increase in prevalence of obesity per state from 1995 to 2001. The states were illustrated in different colors: blue signified more lean populations and bright red indicated states with the highest percentage of obesity. The leanest state was Colorado, in blue, while the heaviest was Mississippi, in bright red.

He continued his lecture: "You may dismiss this information because heavy people have been around for hundreds of years. Obesity and being overweight isn't new. And you are correct. However, it is the quantity of people who are obese that is alarming. In the past, when famines were commonplace, being obese was a sign of wealth. You can see here, in this timeline that I have created, there is the Venus of Wöllendorf. She is the first record of obesity and is thought to be a revered pre-historic idol. This weight signified being well nourished and for a man or lead male it indicated his superiority as a provider for his tribe."

The slide he showed at this point was a brown rock sculpture of a woman. The audience strained to distinguish the features.

"Further down the line are the Baroque paintings of Rubens." He flashed on the screen a painting of a chubby bellied Venus with an adoring Adonis. "And more recently we have our most accepted obese man, Santa Claus of the mid-to-late 1800s." On the screen was a Coca-Cola advertisement of the geriatric, jolly, bearded man holding a glass bottle of cola. The audience chuckled. Dr. Mohr was becoming more relaxed as the audience became more accepting and entertained by what he was telling them.

"So you may wonder why people become obese," he quipped. "It is the simple equation of eating too much and not burning off enough of what you ate. When was the last time anyone here hunted for their food to survive? I mean really to *survive*. And I don't mean baiting a fishing lure to bring dinner to the Winnebago with an already-loaded fridge. When was the last time that any of you has been in a famine?"

He flashed up a picture of a very thin African child covered with flies sucking the minimal fluids from his eyes. The audience became silent.

"What he has, many of you have as well--the hundred or so genes, or blueprints, for your body build. This child is still alive—although barely—because of obesity genes. The famine he is surviving has been going on for a year or two. If he did not have genes potent enough to conserve his energy, he would have been dead a long time ago. He needs those obesity genes to survive. So those of you who are obese are essentially waiting for your famine. The problem for the obese body is the environment in which it lives."

Dr. Mohr proceeded to show the group several slides. To demonstrate how lifestyle contributed to weight, he flashed up an image of a typical, large, suburban house and then an enormous sport-utility vehicle. He then showed the inside of a massive office complex with a maze of grey cubicle dividers. The next slide was a picture of a television. Lastly, he showed a slide with snack foods piled into a pyramid. He called it the "new food pyramid."

The audience giggled for the second time that evening.

"So why should people be concerned? Is it so that everyday Americans can fit into unrealistic Hollywood expectations of what they should look like? No. Obesity is a serious health risk, as well as a burden on the health care system. Obesity causes many health problems including heart disease, diabetes, and cancer. Whether it's arthritis of the spine and knees or lung function, obesity affects almost any organ system," Dr. Mohr explained. He used his laser pointer to go through several slides showing the consequences of obesity.

The audience was pensively silent.

"We adults are not the only ones suffering this scourge of obesity." Dr. Mohr took on a stern and evangelical tone. "It is our children who suffer the most from this." He clicked forward and showed various pictures of obese children with black rectangles over their eyes to protect their identities. The final slides were of an empty school playground, a vending machine and a cartoon rabbit advertising a cereal. "Some schools have recently banned vending machines in school. This is a good start. It's the first time in a long time that we have seen public policies that favored people and not business as usual."

Dr. Mohr's somewhat "leftist" or "liberal" leanings may have become evident though policy initiatives suggested in his talk, but it was becoming fashionable on each side of the ideological spectrum that pushing "junk" foods on children in school was not a good idea. To him, these machines could just as well have been vending cigarettes. Whatever the policy issues, the audience was beginning to get bleary-eyed as a result of Dr. Mohr's proselytizing. Some people were yawning and others had their eyes closed. Many of the laypeople had heard this lecture from their own physicians, albeit not one as elaborate.

"What can be done when people reach the point of obesity?"

The crowd began to come back to life.

"Diet is always an option--but we know how well that works." Dr. Mohr giggled a bit to himself and looked down for a moment. "What we do back home in Maryland is prescribe diets that address the biggest deficits of the patients' current diet. If a person is drinking a gallon of regular soda, then we tell him or her to avoid that through behavioral modification. The goal is ultimately and hopefully to enact lifestyle change."

By this stage the audience had thinned out a bit. People had begun to sneak through the aisles and out the door. He was about fifty minutes into his sixty-minute talk. His watch was nearing four o'clock and that meant the end of another nerve wracking talk. *Just a few more questions from the audience after my conclusion and I will be out the door,* he thought to himself.

"There are medications, but unfortunately, many of my patients cannot take them as they have too many other illnesses that prohibit them or they can't tolerate the side effects. Alternatively, what we can offer is gastric bypass surgery." He showed a cartoon slide by famous medical illustrator Frank Netter of the stomach pre- and post-gastric bypass. "Essentially the stomach is made smaller and the intestines are decreased in length. This is not a cure-all, as a patient can expand the stomach pouch and a person can drink all the liquid calories he or she would like." He didn't divulge further into the surgical procedure, and noticing the time, he abruptly ended the talk. "I know that it's running late, so I want to let you all ask questions."

A very erudite-looking man with wire rimmed glasses, a light blue vest and brown hair parted in the middle asked, "If this is a disease of wealth, why are many of the poor fat? Is it a matter of laziness?"

Dr. Mohr looked at the man as he questioned. He had a brown, bushy mustache that wiggled from side to side to indicate he was talking. It was remarkable to Dr. Mohr that the question was coming from a man who was himself obese and seemed to have a forty-five inch waist crammed into thirty-five-inch slacks. On closer inspection, Dr. Mohr noticed a corner of the man's shirttail was peeking above his waistband as if there was not enough material to cover his belly and stuff into his pants. The question cut among racial and economic lines, but obesity did not discriminate, and grated on Dr. Mohr's sensibilities.

"Well, I think in the United States there is a push in the snack food industry for very cheap foods, and especially drinks, made with high fructose corn syrup. The nation's calorie and carbohydrate intake has increased proportionally to the rate of obesity in this country. These snacks are very cheap, cheaper than healthier foods. Also, foods like vegetables need to be cooked and only taste good when cooked properly. Many poor do not have time to do this, as they are working multiple shifts or taking care of numerous individuals. I think for rich and for poor there is laziness. As I mentioned before this laziness is relative to the amount of food taken in. Thanks to the way snack and fast foods are designed, we fight a losing battle against caloric intake on a daily basis. I hope I am making myself clear." Dr. Mohr tried to make obesity less of a class issue. He was hoping the inquisitor would look down at his own waistline, and by doing so, answer his demographics question.

The blue-vested man sat down, seemingly disappointed that his beliefs had not been reaffirmed. Another man, also with ill-fitting clothes, walked up to a microphone positioned in the hall. His tan colored sport coat and white shirt were too small for his neck and waist and seemed to separate his body into distinguishable parts like on an ant. Blood appeared trapped in his face as if unable to return to the body. Unlike the first man, he was of a sturdy build with broad shoulders and thick arms.

"So do you think that the food companies are trying to make us eat more food or something like that?" he asked. "Do you think that our government is attempting to make us a more obese population?"

"It is in the best interest of food companies to make their foods saltier and sweeter, so that we keep coming back for more. When one food has set the bar high, our bodies become used to it and want more. It takes more of a 'thrill' in terms of food pleasure. I think there is a possibility that the government could—" Dr. Mohr's answer was cut short when the moderator jumped in front of him on the podium.

"I think, Dr. Mohr, we have run out of time. The second-year medical students will be having their lectures in a few minutes. Again, thank you for giving us a very informative lecture," the thin, bald dean of the medical school said into the microphone. He stepped back and put his hands together to initiate the applause for Dr. Mohr. The thinned crowd clapped along with the dean.

Dr. Mohr was relieved. Talks like this drained his energy. All of his stress hormones had just left his body and he nearly collapsed when leaving the stage. He wanted to melt into the floor. He could stop lecturing if he wanted as he'd earned enough in clinical practice. But as happened when a person earned a certain amount of money, the cash became addictive. He was lecturing three to four times monthly and usually earned two thousand dollars per engagement.

"Why don't you come out to the lobby and say hello to some folks?" the dean asked Dr. Mohr with a smile. The dean's head glistened from the heat of the auditorium lamps.

"I'm not feeling too well. Please give anyone outside my contact information and if I can e-mail them, that would be great. I may be coming down with something," Dr. Mohr offered in a quiet tone.

He preferred the formality of the office. He was socially awkward and didn't like meeting strangers *en masse*. He sat backstage behind the drapes on a metal folding chair and caught some of the medical school lecture. The lecture focused on the pharmacology of erectile dysfunction medications. The lecture was followed by a neuroscience talk on synapses that he nearly fell asleep to. It was at this time he was ready to head home. There were only two hours left until his plane left. Syracuse's airport was so small he didn't think it would take too long to get through security. He left through one of the fire doors in the back of the auditorium so as not to run into any curious stragglers from his talk. He had descended the cement stairs when from around the corner he heard, "so the government could be—"

"Sorry, can't talk. Please see the dean for my contact information. I need to catch a plane," Charles mumbled and rushed down the walkway with his computer bag getting tangled in his long, grey trench coat.

A hand grabbed him and he was turned around. It was the man in the tan jacket with broad shoulders whose neck was too big for his shirt.

"Whoa, sorry," the man offered when he saw the stunned look on Charles' face as if he were about to be robbed. He tried to play down the grab. "I just need to know more about your theory."

"Who are you? I need to get to my plane, you know with tighter security and all. My wife is expecting me."

The man who had accosted him was dressed well enough and Dr. Mohr didn't fear he was about to get mugged. *What did he want? He probably needs help losing weight as he's about to burst from his shirt.* Dr. Mohr now wished he had left through the main entry. They were in a walkway that led to the medical school morgue, where donated bodies were delivered and autopsied bodies left for funeral homes. He could smell the formaldehyde coming from inside.

"My name is Dirk Meal. I just want some more information from you." the obese man was shivering in the cold. "We can take our time and I can drive you home, if you miss your flight."

"That's an awfully long ride." Dr. Mohr was very worried about taking a ride with this strange man, although Mr. Meal was shorter than him. He appeared to be very stocky in the mold of a football offensive lineman. *Why would this man want to drive me all the way to Maryland? What **else** does he want to talk about?* "Did my wife send you?" he asked with trepidation. His schedule took him away from home several times a year and caused he and his wife to drift apart. Dr. Mohr was concerned about his wife's suspicions of another woman in his life.

"No, I am…" Dirk tried to get out the words.

"Daria is just a scientist I work with," Dr. Mohr explained quickly before Dirk could finish his sentence.

Dirk was stunned as he looked at the tall lanky man in his early forties. Was this man hiding an affair? Dr. Mohr looked like he had his hand in the cookie jar. Dirk was amazed that this bony and craggy mountain-faced man with a seemingly dry personality had a second love. He remembered from Dr. Mohr's file that his wife's name was Heather. Dirk brushed off Dr. Mohr's embarrassment to reassure the physician. "No, I am with the Federal Bureau of Investigation." Dirk quickly flashed a badge in front of Dr. Mohr, preventing him from getting a good look.

Dr. Mohr disregarded the badge. "Okay, if you don't need to subpoena me, then I will have to catch my plane," Dr. Mohr was relieved the man was not a private investigator hired by his wife, but he was eager to get going. He had always desired more adventure in life, but not ones that took him to jail or an early grave.

"Dr. Mohr, this is official *unofficial* business that my boss, one of the deputy directors at the FBI, is looking into. He needs some info that you can assist us with. He specified you. I would not like to inform Heather of your meeting with Daria but that can be arranged," Dirk sneered. He had very deftly figured out Dr. Mohr was having or was accused of having an affair. He thought he could use this to his advantage in order to get Dr. Mohr to meet with his boss in an orderly, civilized manner.

Dr. Mohr's mind was spinning. What was this all about? *Other than this tryst did I make a deal with the devil? Was I some Don Corleone figure? I paid my taxes on time, right? Is the weight management clinic under investigation for fraud?* He couldn't understand what other wrongdoing he could be involved in. "Okay, I guess a little change of plans is fine. Can I tell my wife that a Dr. Meal would like to talk to me about weight and eating disorders and that I will need to book a later flight?" Dr. Mohr asked sarcastically and with some exasperation. He didn't know what this was about but he was weary. After the talk he felt powerless and decided whatever they had on him should be out in the open.

"Sounds like a good excuse," Dirk said to accommodate him. Dirk liked the idea of being referred to as doctor. He knew his mother would be proud to hear this instead of the usual nondescript 'I work for the government' answer he gave at Thanksgiving.

Dr. Mohr took out his cell phone and dialed. He had woken up Heather, his wife, who sounded drowsy. She asked him what was wrong. He told her quickly but confidently "nothing" and that he would be a little late because of the bizarre Syracuse weather. He didn't want to worry her, no matter what was going to happen to him. She was tired and had heard these excuses before. She let him go. He closed his phone and looked up.

An extended-length black Lincoln Town Car rolled into the driveway near the entrance to the morgue. The car door closest to Dr. Mohr swung open. Dirk gestured with his hand to enter. Dr. Mohr was tempted to throw his computer at Dirk and run. In the back of his mind, he was thinking: *Maybe I am paying for my sins now. Maybe they will take me out to an abandoned field and shoot me in the back of the head. Maybe this is what I deserve.* With this fatalistic view of his life, he lifted his leg, lowered his head, and entered the Town Car, seeing only two legs in navy blue pants in front of him.

Chapter 3

"Dirk, open the trunk and we'll end this ridiculous mission."

The man in the Town Car took up nearly three quarters of the rear bench seat facing the rear window. All of his clothes fit but one knew from looking at him that it took a lot of fabric to cover his girth. He was not only heavy but he, like Dirk Meal, who had gotten in the front passenger seat, had a curvature of his shoulders that indicated that he had worked out. He was bald with grey, well shaven hair on the sides of his head. He was sweating despite the fact the passenger compartment was ice cold. The man reached out his hand to Dr. Mohr.

Dr. Mohr shivered as he got into the car. A pine smell from one of those tiny paper pine tree air fresheners filled the car. Behind the seat of the man in the navy blue suit was a dark-tinted glass divider. Dr. Mohr felt the breeze from the air conditioning and grabbed the outstretched palm. The shake was a mutually soggy one as both men's hands were coated in sweat. Dr. Mohr felt as though he were shaking a baseball mitt as the large man's hands overwhelmed his own. "Cold in here, colder than outside," Dr. Mohr muttered.

"I'm Michael Goldberg, Dr. Mohr, it is very nice to meet you," Goldberg replied in a garbled voice, as if he had marbles in his mouth. He ignored the comment about the climate of the car.

"So, Mr. Goldberg, what does the FBI need a lowly internist that manages weight for? Medicare fraud? I am pretty sure that all my documentation is there. And why would you come all the way out here for this? Do I have some connection to the mob?" Dr. Mohr smiled nervously. He didn't know what to expect. Who would? He believed he was an average man, living a relatively average life.

"Please, no, it's nothing like that, and please call me Mike. So calm down, we have a long ride to Maryland and we can talk about things," Mike smiled and cracked the window open a bit. He reached the top pocket of his suit jacket and pulled out a box of Marlboro Lights. He tilted the box toward Dr. Mohr. One cigarette stuck out of the pack when the car started to move.

Dr. Mohr was tempted to take the cigarette. "It would seem hypocritical for a physician, who has seen the ravages of people's vices getting them into trouble, to take a cigarette."

"Relax, relax. I just want some information. Let's say a consultation. No biggie. But I should maybe look into your billing... heh, heh," Mike joked. He talked with his hands and while he spoke it looked like was swimming with a breast stroke.

"I think this is extreme. You could have made an appointment," Dr. Mohr sighed, exhausted, even more spent than just from the lecture. He didn't like the comment about the billing. He knew Mike was joking but he understood that any irregularity could carry some severe penalties. In the office, he made sure to dot every "I" and cross every "T" when it came to billing. He just wanted to be home. He wanted to be in a nice warm bed, not shivering in this limousine. He didn't even want to think anymore. There was no hard inquisition but he was ready to tell them anything they wanted to know. *Couldn't this guy have made an appointment? Stupid FBI, shouldn't they be tracking illegals or Osama? Why are they picking on me? Are these guys really the FBI? Just let me give you the information you need and I can be on my way.*

"You're a real funny guy. Maybe I should come to you for controlling my own weight," Mike responded to Dr. Mohr's appointment request. His jowls shook as he talked. "On another somewhat-related topic, you know there is an election happening, soon. Looks like the president's popularity is way up there. He's got the whole rally-the-troops thing going. He's also riding the wave of

'You can't change philosophy in the middle of a war.' He's cracking down on all sorts of things. You know he is the most physically fit president ever. He even made obesity an issue of national security. A small issue but better than ignoring it. Do you believe that? Fatsos like me and al-Qaeda are in the same category. I really think with this he's off of his gourd. Anyway, you know his Secretary of Agriculture is going to be the next vice-president, replacing the dumbass that currently holds the office. Did you ever meet the new potential VP? Gordon Irving. He's a nice guy. He will make a good VP and maybe eventually president. I could swear you guys have crossed paths. He is a little older than you. Twelve years, but I thought you knew him," Michael goaded him for the association as sweat started to come through the armpits of his blue silk suit.

"No, not that I can recall now. Was that all you needed to know?" Dr. Mohr didn't even process the request. He had heard of Mr. Irving's name on CNN but he didn't realize there was any connection with himself. He could feel Mike trying to push him into knowing this man. *But why?*

"Why don't you have a little something to eat? How about some apple pie? We even have some ice cream and whipped cream. Then we can talk more about some of your theories of government and how we bureaucrats have caused obesity." Mike dug the pie out of the mini-fridge. He was trying to get information from Dr. Mohr but at the same time not putting thoughts in his head. He awkwardly tried to cut the pie with a plastic knife with his right hand while holding the base with his left. Crust was getting all over the black interior. Mike put a slice on a plate on top of the mini-fridge and continued to gather the ingredients to construct his pie *a la mode*.

Dr. Mohr inhaled the sweet apple smell. It was a familiar aroma that was found in his parents' tiny suburban Chicago address when he was a boy, at a time when his parents were still together. It was a welcome treat when he was young. The pie was the 'icing on the cake' when his father came home from his job in sales. He was always gone for days, sometimes weeks at a time. The pie in front of him made him remember the good times. He took the pie and watched as Mike struggled to get a second piece out.

"Aww, shit, come on guys," Mike knocked on the glass behind him. The Town Car had hit a large pothole and the large man had knocked a large, sticky piece of pie onto his own very white shirt. The pie left a yellow stain. He managed to get control of the food and placed what looked to Dr. Mohr like one-third of the pie onto his plate.

"Didn't you have a summer job at Washington University?" Mike continued his inquisition with a face full of food in his mouth. Mike hoped the light bulb would go off.

Dr. Mohr could barely make out what was asked of him through Mike's garbled, food-filled speech but he believed it had something to do with the little bit of research he did in the 1970s at Washington. It seemed a vague reference to him, something that happened almost thirty years ago. He didn't remember the details of his 10th grade summer project but it had inspired him to pursue medicine and eventually obesity care. Prior to his arrival, the lab had been given a sample of several compounds to test on mice. They were taste additives. His job was to help tend to the mice and write down observations with the Chinese post-doctoral fellow. Of the hundred or so compounds, a couple of them really stimulated the mice to eat almost uncontrollably. The mice would eat and eat, and he remembered the sound of them voraciously chewing the brown pellets filled with the compound. He also remembered how they would squeak incessantly in a depressive fit when he took away their food.

Through these experiments, he gained an appreciation for the way man could manipulate nature and behavior. John Stevenson, an expert in feeding behavior, ran this laboratory and mentored him. In college, he struggled with the decision of being a pure scientist or becoming a physician. He had spent some time in his uncle's gastroenterology office. He liked the idea of using science to help people. After medical school he did try to return to basic science but, as evidenced by the Syracuse lecture, the idea of presenting his ideas in front of a highly critical close knit group unnerved him.

The memories of these days reminded him of the family connections that had led him to becoming a physician. The physician uncle was on his mother's side. This was the professional side of the family. His father on the other hand had grown up in a poorly educated family that lived in a trailer park in Oklahoma. His father had great admiration for his mother's scholarly family. His father himself had no great knack for books. Dr. Mohr's father had told his son that education was the way to have a good family life. He was dissuaded not to follow in his father's footsteps as a salesman concerned with quotas and orders from upper management. The elder Mohr gave his son every opportunity, paid for his college and medical school. He also got him the summer job at the lab. His father's boss at AG-USA, a major animal feed and corn supplier, was a good friend of Dr. Stevenson.

"Yes, it was a while ago. I know. But did your time over there have anything to do with some of your current theories on how everyone got so fat--I mean, obese?" Mike asked.

"No, what do you mean? There's a genetic predisposition to obesity, and in hard times or famine, obese people are better able to survive, at least, compared to people that can eat anything they want and still not gain a pound. We live in a world where food is plentiful and jobs take little if any energy. People naturally want to eat until they are stuffed," Dr. Mohr said, ready to give his lecture again.

"It is amazing how policies can change the way we look and how we act," Mike smiled. He wanted Dr. Mohr to get the punchline without him having to tell the joke. His bosses wanted to make sure that Dr. Mohr was as ignorant as he appeared right now. Mike continued to pick at the scab until it bled answers.

"Oh yes, well, taking physical education out of our schools and putting fast food in them would affect the way a population would look. And I agree the increasing reliance on motorized transport that increases commute times appears to decrease the time for exercise," Dr. Mohr explained with more ease. He was becoming less stressed and was getting into a groove with his obesity talk. However at the same time, the conversation did little to energize him as the pie had started to make him feel sleepy. Everything said up until now was hypothetical and the lack of concrete fact made it difficult for Dr. Mohr to keep up with the conversation in his current state of exhaustion.

"Are you of the same opinion as these authors that the government is directly contributing to obesity?" Michael asked with some conviction and pointed to articles that laid next to him including one with the title "Your Government and Your Waistline." He was again trying to push the right button to get a particular admission from Dr. Mohr but he wasn't getting close. Mike was getting tired as well. This was nothing new as even though the hour was late, he was tired most of the time. Mike's weight had caused him to have a disorder called sleep apnea that kept him oxygen deprived at night and subsequently tired all day.

Last year a journalist had come to Dr. Mohr's home in Maryland. They'd sat in his sun room and talked about obesity and its causes. The man spouted some wild ideas about key people in the government that had a vested interest in making America obese. He had conducted a few interviews for local television stations with the journalist and although the man's ideas were fanciful Dr. Mohr couldn't remember him that well. What he did remember was that the journalist's argument sounded like paranoia but now, in light of his current conversation, he began to believe the man may have been correct. Although he felt the government policies could increase obesity, they did so in the setting of an obesity-predisposed genetic background that could not adapt. There didn't seem to be any one looming person that was the root of obesity. *Did Goldberg believe I worked with the one man that singlehandedly caused the obesity epidemic? Was it someone that I knew?*

"There are lots of those authors. They're not scientists and many of the journalists are just looking for the next big scandal. I don't believe that any one person was trying to get the American people to become fat. It was probably a side effect of certain growth policies, an excess of food supply overall, food companies jockeying for customers with sweeter and saltier foods," Dr. Mohr pointed out confidently.

"What about your work on corn syrup in Dr. Stevenson's lab?" Mike insisted, growing frustrated. He was tempted to reveal details about who he was working for to get the answer he was seeking, as he was exhausted at two o'clock in the morning and he needed to go to the bathroom. He loved ice cream but it gave him horrendous gas. Fortunately for him and his travelling companion, any of his emissions were masked by the malodorous smell of the northern New Jersey chemical plants they were passing.

"Are you suggesting some conflict of interest? I think it would be pretty weird to say some college sophomore who was basically a dishwasher in a lab, contributed to obesity so that he could reap the rewards in clinical practice several years later. Mr. FBI man, you have a pretty good imagination." By now Dr. Mohr thought the questioning was just silly.

"No, ahh, dammit." Mike knocked on the limousine divider window with a gold class ring on his pinky finger. "Are we near the Perth exit?"

"Yes boss," the driver answered in a gruff voice.

"Okay let's stop here at the Amtrak station. Dirk, open the trunk and we'll end this ridiculous mission. Awww, goddamn cramps," Mike groaned, grabbing his stomach.

"Are you all right?" Dr. Mohr asked. He didn't like to ask as if there was something wrong as he might have to act upon it. He hated emergency situations. He had chosen a specialty involving chronic illness where things moved at a snail's pace for just this reason.

Mike shook his head in affirmation of relative well-being. The car stopped and he opened the door, crawled out and slammed it behind him. Mike walked back to the trunk.

Dr. Mohr heard the squeak of the hinges as Mike fully opened it. He heard a front door open and slammed also which he believed must have been Dirk. Dirk's footsteps also approached the trunk.

"Dirk, take care of Dr. Mohr and let's catch the 2:30 for DC. I gotta find a bathroom."

Dr. Mohr heard the conversation through a crack in the rear passenger window. He was a little bit scared. *What are they doing in the trunk? Are they going to shoot me or something?* All the confidence he had just a few minutes ago was now gone. Sweat beaded on his brow despite the car still being very cold. The trunk closed with a thud and he felt the rear end of the car bounce. He was too tired to rationalize or make any escape plan when the door opened right by him. He jumped.

"Here you go," Dirk said and handed him a blanket. "Ian, the driver, will take you back home. Why don't you get some sleep. We are sorry for surprising you. Mr. Goldberg or I will be in touch with you if we have any further questions."

Dr. Mohr took the blanket in his hand and unfolded it. He didn't say a word.

"Ian, turn the heat up back here. It's freezing!" Dirk commanded Ian and shut the door.

Dr. Mohr curled up in the blanket and fell asleep quickly. A shy, introverted individual, this kind of event was too strange for him. He just wanted to go back to bed and pretend this hadn't happened. In fact, maybe he was already asleep and would wake up in his own bed.

"Hey doc, if you need—" Ian stopped mid-sentence. He looked back and heard Dr. Mohr snoring. Ian raised the partition window and continued down the New Jersey Turnpike.

Chapter 4

"Tell your pointy headed friends to find something else to write about. I don't need to be diggin' up old graves."

Willie climbed out of his old Lincoln. The green paint was marred by rust spots. The water snuck in at the key hole and bubbled the paint underneath as if the keyhole was crying. The white vinyl top was grey and cracked, revealing the felt insulation underneath. The wear was on Willie as well. His bushy Afro was now trimmed closely around his ears. The top of his hair was thinning, especially at the hairline. He still had broad shoulders but it was accompanied by a small, middle aged belly.

"Yo man, you need anything?" a teenager asked as he walked by in a black sweatshirt and jeans.

Willie smelled a near overpowering cologne emanating from the boy. "Don't you have to get to school? I'll give you yesterday's paper if you'd like. Reading will do you good."

"Naw, man. I got business to attend to," the boy replied with a visible gold cap in his incisor. The boy turned around and walked across the street catty-corner from Rock Bottom's. He joined other teenagers on the corner. Periodically a car would stop for a few seconds in front of the boys, and then rush off.

Willie looked at the sky as the first bits of orange lit the heavens. He shook his head, thinking it was too early to be dealing drugs. Willie bent down to open the steel grate that covered the plate glass of his newspaper stand. He could smell urine emitting from the abandoned bar next door. He felt a slight breeze as he picked up a bale of the *Washington Post* and another of *New York Daily News*. *What are these kids thinking? These stupid kids.* He remembered his cousin, El, lying in the casket at the church. The coffin smelled of perfume and formaldehyde. The funeral director had left a dimpled smile for him to enter the afterlife. People were whimpering and wailing. The loudest was his cousin's mother who was arm-in-arm with her third husband/boyfriend, the Reverend Jonathan Mays. He always thought it was so ironic that the dead got the VIP treatment. If El had half of this love during his lifetime, he wouldn't have needed comfort in drugs.

Many years after his cousin's death, El's son was caught in the familiar cycle for this neighborhood as the streets coddled and shaped him. Though, unlike his "user" father, he became a kingpin of the local corner. He would stop by in his cream-colored Escalade, trimmed in optional equipment worth more than the car. Willie would watch the Boss check in on his employees, exchange money, and drop off drugs. If he was a legitimate business man, he could see himself building an empire with his second cousin. The Boss preferred Willie as he knew him now, a distant figure, a part of the scenery, and a remnant of a neighborhood trying to be functional replete with nuclear families and engaged and invested neighbors.

The day passed as usual. Elementary school children would come by Willie's newsstand and get a soda and some chips at around 2:30 P.M. Then they would pass by their drug-dealing future employers. Spring smelled very similar to other months with cars and trucks rolling by and very little greenery to quell the smog. The air was still somewhat chilly, but it didn't warrant the oversized sweatshirts worn by all the schoolchildren. A little closer to three o'clock, Willie saw a cluster of boys gathering around something or someone. Between the dealers, they were tossing something or somebody between them. The man appeared a foot shorter than the others at the rim of the circle. When the circle widened a bit, he could see a strange-looking white man being tossed from person to person like a game of hot potato. The man had oddly spiked hair that curled towards the tips. His white skin was emphasized by his dark rimmed glasses. He wore a faded denim jacket with brown corduroy pants. On his shoulder was a pea green shoulder bag that appeared to hold a laptop or books. Willie thought it was just another university student that didn't have enough cash for his drugs. A few more tosses by the boys and he began to notice a drop of blood running from the nose of the man. Willie broke away from the newsstand and slowly stepped toward the corner. *I shouldn't get involved. They are my neighbors who mutually and tenuously keep each other around. If I call the cops or interfere with their goings-on, I may get killed and they get sent to jail. Any hope of a renaissance in this neighborhood dies with me..* This thought had often prevented him from diving in to break up fights. He was only ten feet away from the group now. He contemplated just being a spectator.

"Nice book about fat-asses," a tall boy with a scar above his right eyebrow spat.

"Yo, Judah, this yo' handbook," a shorter boy in a red sweatshirt ribbed.

The heavyset Judah smiled and nodded with a face full of golden teeth.

"How 'bout this fat-ass book up your skinny little white ass, fuckin' snitch," Scarface fired back.

"Hey!" Willie yelled. He didn't know what it would sound like. It resonated in his head like a gun fired in a tunnel. *What the hell am I doing?* He had a nice store and was able to keep up the payments and feed himself too. He didn't have to be a hero. He especially did not need to sacrifice his hide for a crack head. He knew that these drug-dealing kids had no forethought of the greater impact of their careers on the community. But he jumped in not only to protect a potential addict but to prevent a worse fate for the young criminals after a murder.

"This your customer? Keep him outta our store," Scarface hissed.

The boy with the red sweatshirt who held the little man by the back of his jacket threw him forward. The little man landed chest first on the pavement. The gang turned their backs and walked off when their toy was taken away. The man's arms were shaking as he reached for the pavement to stand. Willie grabbed him by the arm. His upper lip was smeared with dried blood and his right eyeglass lens had a small fracture.

"Just a misunderstanding. That'll teach me to ask for directions," he swept the dirt from his pants.

Willie saw a small wet spot in the crotch of his pants. He didn't reply to his statement or the stain. The man looked like an alien visiting *his* Earth.

"Are you Willie Barnes? The one of the Washington newsstand right there?" the man asked and pointed at his store.

"And if I was, what would you want with me?" Willie countered, hoping that this strange fellow would say his piece and leave him alone.

"Jason Lieberman, Mr. Barnes. I thought we could chew the fat," Jason stuck his hand out to his savior and smiled but Willie ignored the gesture. He then picked up a random paper on the stands and put it on the counter to pay, possibly to spur his conversation.

"Long way to get a black newspaper," Willie coughed and eyed the price on *The Heritage Daily* and rang it up behind the counter.

"Oh." Jason said embarrassed about his choice. "And some of these," Jason handed him a bag of pork rinds.

"Two-fifty. Please recommend your friends come over for their pork rinds and Afro-American literature, but make sure they beware of the neighbors across the street." Willie smiled sarcastically and bagged the items.

"Thanks for the help with your boys over there," Jason offered, trying to make a connection.

"They're far from *my* boys and I would recommend that if you have any pertinent business to take care of, do it and be gone before they feel like coming back here and release their teenage angst on you." Willie's voice became sterner and his eyes grew wider.

"The reason I am here is to ask about your work in the Stevenson lab," Jason said quickly.

"Why do you want to bring up that old shit? That was nearly twenty-five, thirty years ago. I don't need to be part of some graduate student project. Get lost. Go on. Tell your pointy headed friends to find something else to write about. I don't need to be diggin' up old graves." Willie's voice got louder with each sentence. He started to come from behind the counter and pointed to the main road.

"Just a few questions. This isn't a grad student project. We can make a difference here." Jason increased his voice to keep up but backed away from the counter.

"Listen--a twenty-year-old student making some extra bucks in a chemistry lab, in my book, does not constitute a story. Now get the fu— outta my face." Willie caught himself from saying the entire f-word. In his old age, he had tried to eliminate swear words from his vocabulary, though in this conversation, it was losing the battle. He had also eyed a couple of first graders coming home from school across the street. He continued to point in the direction of the main road encouraging Jason's egress.

Jason was a bit intimidated as a stranger in a strange land. He was afraid the dealers would come back to tell him to keep away, but he knew he had to touch a nerve to get to the hidden reserve of knowledge underneath. "Mr. Barnes, I am an accomplished author and I think we may be able to turn the tide in the coming presidential election." Jason flashed the back cover of a book at Willie called *One Nation Under Oil.* The book was a glossy orange color and on the bottom was Jason's picture.

Willie looked at the back cover and the picture that looked vaguely like Jason except he had straight hair and no glasses. "Yeah, so what, I know your book. I own a newsstand. I *read* the *New York Times* literature section. What do you want to do, make me Movie of the Week?"

"I think you may be a key to this story. The story of how we as a nation became fat, just from a few wheels and deals from the lobbying seat. You were part of that and you were on the ground floor. You helped create the crack for disease to crawl through. Everybody needs to eat. Black and white, rich and poor, we all need to eat. Those experiments that you did in the seventies were the key," Jason insisted, pleading with him.

"Who do you think I am? Pablo Escobar? Look across the street. Those are the real villains! I *ain't* no dealer. People do need to eat. I helped make people's food more enjoyable. It was more than thirty-something years ago. It's dead and gone," Willie whispered the last part softly. He looked at the ground and scrubbed his foot against the concrete floor.

"Mr. Barnes, you aren't the villain, just a small but key piece of the puzzle. You were on the ground floor of something very big. Something that went up to the very highest seats of government. You could help right the ship or at least bring down some of the forces that have created the mess you have here. Look at the people here." Jason opened his palm and made a 180 degree turn toward the street. "You look like you have been keeping up with yourself. But what about some of the others? You've got some very big people here. And they are falling apart at the seams. They have diabetes and they are going blind and they are losing their limbs. The weight is taking its toll and they can't stop eating. Maybe it's the disease but maybe it's what's in the food. Maybe it's how food is marketed, Maybe it's poor choices. But there was an event sometime in the mid-seventies that increased obesity all over this country. I think that event, or predominant event, is linked to some of the scientists you worked with."

"Hey man, when are the aliens coming to probe your ass? You think it's that simple? Just one thing, huh?" Willie chuckled to himself.

The two first graders came across the street to get some fake juice drinks. One was a boy in a jean jacket. His pants struggled to contain his waist. His friend was a girl in a pink shirt and grey sweatshirt. The pink shirt couldn't cover her belly. She was very large for her age and height and must have weighed one hundred pounds.

"I don't have enough facts but there are people that may be selected to future offices that could have caused this. There are people who benefited richly from ordinary citizens getting fat. Now they may be controlling the country." Jason turned toward the children who had just reached the curb closest to the news-stand. "This information will influence future generations. Look at them. In five years they'll barely be able to breathe. In fifteen years they'll be in one of those little Rascal mobility scooters. You're not in trouble here. I'm trying to get you to help me take the big guys down. Maybe even make up for the past."

"What do you know about me?" Willie frowned and then looked at the children.

"Just these, mister," said the little boy oblivious to the adult discussion. He reached his hand above the counter to get a packet of cheese puffs and a candy bar.

"No, go on. This stuff ain't for you. Run home to your mom. This stuff is no good for you. Get going. This is grown-up talk going on in here. Go." Willie raised his voice and motioned to the children to leave. The guilt began to grow in him as these chubby children tried to buy junk food from him.

"What, is my money not good here? C'mon, when did I need an ID to buy cheese puffs?" the boy tested him.

"I said git. Now respect your elders and get out of my store. Not today. Go." Willie demanded.

"C'mon, Russell, let's go," the little girl lisped.

Russell grabbed her by the hand and they ran out of the stand. Jason held up his hands and stepped out of their way.

"Hey, don't let me stop you from doing business as usual. Anyway, maybe I was barking up the wrong tree," Jason turned to walk away.

"Man, wait a minute," Willie sighed. Chasing the kids away did nothing to hide the guilt that Jason uncovered.

Jason turned around and saw Willie smile.

"You think we can fix some of this stuff? I've seen too much hurting people around here. Old men and women in their little scooters dying slowly. If I can help, or if I have one chance to make a small difference that would be great," Willie asked.

"It is up to the general public to make a conscious effort to take control of their bodies. But maybe what we know may change government regulations or remove the people that want to keep the status quo," Jason said to encourage him.

"So is there any risk besides me digging up my past?" questioned Willie.

"You get the usual fist-shaking by the people who you denounce but all in all it's very civil. Although many of the people we talk about may be coming up for election next year. Guess it just depends on how desperate they are." Jason shrugged his shoulders and smiled. Jason had talked in inspirational terms to Willie but what he cared most about was his next big paycheck. He had played well to the liberal left and was hoping to score even larger sales. He knew very little of the risks of irking the higher echelons of government during a crucial election time.

"I need to show you something. I know it's there but I haven't been back to see it for quite a while. An old friend of mine that got me through those years you spoke of, and now she's been put out to pasture. When are you free?" Willie shook his head in disbelief at what he himself was suggesting. His life was currently stable but he missed the days of being called Neptune and of thinking of the future. This could be a way to rekindle the young, goal-oriented Willie.

Jason was confused, "Is this another witness? Ideally. I'd like to get this book done soon. I have got a lot of evidence already. All I need to do is corroborate the stories. Can I meet this person tomorrow and you can tell me the details of your work with the Stevenson lab?"

"I think you'll like what we find in this witness. My calendar is free tomorrow. News business has been slow since the Internet. They won't miss me. Here's where I need you to meet me." Willie wrote down the directions and handed Jason the paper.

Jason walked away from the stand and looked at the address. He was perplexed at the location of the witness but asked no further questions of Willie so as not to perturb him to an extent that would prevent him from telling the story he wanted.

Chapter 5

"I don't care for breakfast. This is all so imaginary."

Daria hurriedly buttoned her white silk blouse. She fumbled with the buttons because she was shaking. She liked his awkwardness, his intelligence, and his quiet demeanor. He was nothing like her long-dismissed fiancé, Ben, who was the typical frat boy; a cool guy that was boisterous most of the time, especially with alcohol on board.

The contrast with Dr. Charles Mohr had made her jettison the frat boy a few years ago. *Maybe Charles is what I really want,* was what she initially thought. Now, she struggled with passion and practicality.

"Hey, why are you awake? I thought we could have breakfast in bed. Awwwh," Dr. Mohr yawned. His chest was exposed and one of his legs was hanging outside the sheet.

"Charlie, why do we keep seeing each other? Why do we keep living separate lives?" Daria demanded while slipping on her navy blue skirt. She looked at him. She asked these questions because she wanted a semblance of a normal life--but not necessarily with him. He was ten years older than her. She was thirty-two and she didn't believe that Charles would be a future father to her children as she didn't believe he would leave his family. But he was just more put together than many of the single men that she had met since she broke off her engagement. Meeting people had been so much easier when she met Ben. There were no responsibilities in college, no budgets, and no limits to knowing a boyfriend. The problem with Ben was that he had remained in college mode six years after leaving school. She felt a huge pressure to settle down. Her list of single friends had dwindled and she saw her future as an aimless pinball bouncing from one pointless relationship to another.

She met Charles at a food convention six years ago. He had given a talk on obesity that she thought might be different than the chemistry lectures she had been going to. She thought it was a provocative lecture. He was not part of the corporate world that she had literally been a part of since she was a Master's student. She liked the altruistic nature of what he was studying. He portrayed the obese as victims of nature, genetics and environment. It was surprising that a man who was so thin and in good shape could be so empathetic to them.

As with most of the country, she was taught by the media to think the Hollywood-brainwashed idea of thinness was the norm. All of the men she had dated were muscular and taut. Even Ben, with his constant drinking parties, remained thin and buff. She herself took pride in her thinness. She didn't have to work too hard at it either, as she was known to eat at McDonald's once a week. Before the lecture, she'd believed obese people had no self-respect and were lazy. Charles made an argument about the corporate and national influence on obesity that was profound and compelling. *Could food producers be to blame? Had the government developed policies to create this problem intentionally? Were economic benefits to the few meant to cause an economic downturn for the many? Was she working for people who contributed to this?* She wanted to know what Dr. Mohr believed her and her company's role was in making people heavy. This was her bright-eyed vision many years ago.

She received all the answers to these questions soon after they met. She was paid nearly two-and-a-half times her salary by a food additive company to keep an eye on her lover. Their relationship was predicated on a sandwich piled sky-high with lies. The point of her spying was never evident to her, as she never found that he had any hard evidence for his corporate-blame theories. She gave her semi-annual and any additional surprise reports to Sheldon Hairston, her boss. Despite her deceit, she kept the fairytale ideal of settling down with Charles in her head and this motivated her to be with him. She kept her options open dating other men while seeing Charles. They were less intellectually stimulating but more physically attractive to her. Charles had the right combination of looks and intellect that she believed would create an idyllic relationship. At thirty-two and by no means too old to have children, she still felt behind the eight ball and craved a real lifelong bond. So she looked at him with his hand out seeking her own to hold and thought, *I have to end this charade with a married man.*

"I don't care for breakfast. This is all so imaginary," she snorted toward the ground as she continued to get dressed.

"We've talked about this. It's complicated. I have explained to you many times about my wife and kids. This is, I guess, only a here-and-now relationship," Charles explained, trying to quantize human interaction into long-term and short-term possibilities.

"Exactly, they're real and I'm—" her voice broke as she started to cry "—not," she squealed. She sat back down on the bed.

Charles sat up in the bed and put his hands on her shoulders. "Hey, hey, hey. We both knew what this relationship was about when we started it so many years ago."

Tears ran down Daria's cheeks filled with dark black mascara. She looked into the mirror. "Why do I put up with this? Look at me. I am a professional, attractive woman. I'm not one of the pigs you talk about. You have so much empathy for these jerks that you don't even know. What about me? Obviously I am unreal to you. I'm just an object. Someone you can talk shop with and then fuck. I have to go." Daria broke from Charles' massaging hands.

"Wait, Daria…" Charles insisted, but he did not make much of a motion to stop her.

Daria whipped her suit jacket off of the desk chair in the room and slammed the door behind her.

Charles lay back in bed and a tear started to form in his right eye. He retraced their steps from the night before. They met at the New Orleans airport, went to an obesity meeting and talked to various colleagues and then to a fancy cocktail party at Louis XVI in the French Quarter. Her smile glistened in an echo with the wine crystal. They had a lot to drink and moved on to the Cat's Meow, where she sang her lungs out to Peter Frampton's *Baby I Love Your Way*. He thought they had fun and couldn't foresee her outburst in any way. *Maybe she will get over this in a while. She knew what their relationship was all about. It will all be okay.*

A red light flashed on the phone. It was his wife and he had forgotten to do his usual on-the-road ten o'clock check-in.

Daria walked diagonally from the Holiday Inn to a small park across the street from the convention center. The sun was just peeping over the large horizontal structure. Little sparrows were circling around her, thinking she had their breakfast. The air smelled of garbage which had recently been hauled away.

She sat on one of the black iron benches. She was still weeping and wiping her face with the sleeves of her navy blue suit jacket. Her cell phone rang. The caller ID showed an area code that was unfamiliar to her. She flipped open her tiny phone.

"Hey, Sheldon here. Daria, we may need your help to stay close to Dr. Mohr. We have new—"

She screamed into the phone, "Fuck you, Sheldon!" She pressed the hang-up button so hard, wanting to force it through the phone. The phone did not break and it rang again with the same number. This time she opened it and turned the ringer off.

*   *   *

Charles didn't speak to Daria during the rest of the time in New Orleans. He took a late evening flight from there to Macon, Georgia. He got in late at his mother-in-law's house and fell asleep on the couch so as not to wake anyone. The sleepy town with its pre-Civil War charm was a place of unlocked car- and home doors so it was easy for him to sneak in.

In the morning, the sound of whimpering on the front porch awakened him. He looked at the white boarded ceiling. The smell of freshly brewed coffee filled the room. The sun had made its way into the living room. Charles heard a shuffling, slipper-laden step and saw his mother-in-law with a blank expression crouched over him.

"You best go onto the porch and remedy the situation," she ordered.

"Huh?" Charles tried to get his bearings.

"You heard me, now git," she pulled away the multicolored knit blanket that he had covered himself with.

"All right," he sat up in the chair and rubbed his eyes. He looked at his watch which read five after seven. Unscrewing the fob on his watch, he moved the hands to five after eight Eastern Standard Time, still early on a Sunday morning. His shirt tails were undone under the sport-jacket he was wearing, when he went to get a cup of coffee from the kitchen. He drank his cup and looked at the black and white photo on the wall. It was a picture of his wife's grandparents. They were sitting on a porch in rocking chairs. Her grandmother looked to be in her sixties but by her appearance, but her wife had told him at a previous visit that they were actually in their early forties. Both she and her husband were riddled with facial lines as they smiled. Time and effort did not treat her well. At the corner of her mouth was a corncob pipe.

"If I was her, I would have waited for you on the porch last night and then I would have blown a hole the size of Daddy's pick-up right through your belly," his mother-in-law mumbled.

"What?" Charles asked. But his mother-in-law had already shuffled into her bedroom and closed the door. Charles shrugged his shoulders and walked to the front screen door.

On a white wicker chair, Heather was sitting in the fetal position holding a blue coffee mug that had inscribed on it Eastern Shore Weight Management Centers. She was sniffling and tears ran down her cheeks. A lump grew in Charles' throat and his heart sunk.

He remembered the first time that they met. He had just completed a night of medicine ward call at Georgetown hospital. The call there was very tough as a resident; not only had to take care of their patients' medical conditions but also had to transport them for x-rays and perform all the necessary blood work. After his shift, he wanted to grab a cup of coffee in Dupont circle near his apartment and veg on the couch. Although he had a strong desire to sleep, he wanted to stay awake so that his clock wasn't thrown off. When he got to the coffee shop, he looked around for a seat but the place was packed with Washington University students. He noticed one girl sitting at a table talking to her friend.

She was the most beautiful woman he had laid eyes on with or without the weariness of call. She was tiny and couldn't have been taller than four-foot-eleven. All of her clothes, especially the WU sweatshirt she was wearing, looked too big for her. He felt a little strange looking at her, as he thought for a minute that she was underage. Her friend was wearing a green baseball hat with sorority letters on it and looked to be in her early twenties. This was reassuring to him. In mid-conversation Heather turned and smiled at him. He must have looked pathetic. His straight brown hair was in a "bed head" state, as he was never one to make himself up post-call. He hadn't even shaved that morning. His scrub pants were a few sizes too big and they were tied to his waist as if he was wearing a potato sack.

Within a few minutes, her friend had left and since there were no other seats available, he thought in his dazed post call bravado this would be as good a time as any to meet a strange girl.

"Anyone sitting here?" Charles asked.

"Oh, ah, no, go on ahead," Heather said nervously. She liked meeting new people and would start conversations with random people in grocery stores, bus stops, and galleries.

"Sorry about my appearance," Charles apologized. He was also concerned about his odor as he had worked nearly thirty hours straight without a shower. She didn't seem to notice. He looked at the art history book in front of her. He started talking to her about the American Sublime and his favorite painter Albert Beirstadt. She couldn't comment on that genre but she went on about her favorite modern artists Jackson Pollock and Hans Hofman. He didn't understand most of what she was saying but listened because it was such different conversation. It wasn't the constant whining of his fellow residents about such and such a fellow resident, or intern or patient. Their conversation lasted for three hours and within a few days they went out on their first date. The dates multiplied, they became engaged and eventually married. They had two children; one was now fourteen and the other was five.

When he looked out the screen door, he didn't know if the novelty about her had worn off. She still had those "baby fat" cheeks that gave her such a youthful appearance. She had aged much better than her grandmother. The door creaked as Charles went out onto the porch. The sun glistened off of the magnolia tree in the front yard. The buds were near breaking. On the other side of the porch, a slight breeze was shaking the Spanish moss that hung from a small oak tree. She continued to stare out at the street as he faced her.

"Morning," he offered with trepidation.

She didn't say anything but sniffled.

"What's wrong, honey?" Charles pleaded.

"You know what's wrong." Heather replied.

"I just have meetings you know. You married an expert in a field. Unfortunately, that's what I do to help pay the bills. Sometimes I don't get to talk to you when I am at these meetings." Charles explained.

"If you mean meetings, do you mean her? I smell her perfume on you. I see the lipstick on your collar. She is not imaginary and she is not a 'meeting'," she yelled. Heather didn't know exactly who the other woman was just that there was one. He was always away and the curt conversations while he was on trips or working long hours at his office deteriorated their relationship.

"There is nothing going on. I love you and I think about you and the kids whenever I am out. I do my song-and-dance routine at these stupid conventions for you guys," Charles pleaded.

"Why didn't you call on Friday? I left a message at your hotel when you didn't call. I was worried. But why should I worry, I just look like I have egg on my face. You just humiliate me when I worry about you because you are with some other woman," Heather croaked between her tears.

"Hmmh. Heather, I would not ever want you to feel that way. I am sorry," Charles said and looked at the navy blue cushion covered in bright pink lilies.

"You need to stop seeing whoever she is and when we get home we need to get some counseling, otherwise, this will not work out for me," Heather countered and dried some of her tears on the Mexico t-shirt she was wearing.

"All right, I'll do whatever you want. I just don't want to see you cry," Charles agreed. For Charles, his feelings for his wife were related to distance.

He felt as close as crossed fingers to her in her presence but away from her she was his distant past.

"Mornin,' y'all," a crew-cut, grey-haired, elderly white man yelled from the porch across the street. The man stuck his arm up and waved. He wore the local traditional outfit a red plaid shirt with a denim jumper.

Charles stuck up his hand and smiled. He then stood up and opened the screen door for Heather to go inside. "We'll talk more about it when we get back to home, all right? How is your Mom doing?" he asked to change the subject.

Heather stood up and looked at him. In his disheveled appearance she saw the man she met in the coffee shop. She smiled for a quick second. "Her symptoms wax and wane. The meds for the Parkinson's make her delusional on occasion, otherwise, she's okay," Heather said softly as she entered the house.

Charles waved at the man rocking away across the street and closed the screen door.

*   *   *

Daria and Charles first met at a convention in Denver in March. There was still ample season for any of the conventioneers to hit the slopes when meetings were over. The meetings were held in a hotel by the airport. If you were not doing a ski excursion and had not rented a car, you were trapped as the airport was several miles away from town. However, it was a good year to be trapped anywhere in Denver. People everywhere had a glow about them. John Elway had led the Denver Broncos to a Super Bowl win and there were dark blue and orange colored objects everywhere to commemorate the achievement.

The convention was a meeting of different food companies that were showcasing their newest food creations. Frito-Lay was displaying its newest chip. Kidder-Hunt was touting McDonalds' new tastier and meatier sandwich. Other "behind the scenes" food developers were there too, who boasted about additives they had created and placed in these foods that made the eating experience extraordinary.

Daria worked for one of these covert companies. The biochemistry department of Rutgers University had a cooperative PhD program with AGWorld.

AGWorld paid her tuition, she got a job when she got out and the company had at least a four-year commitment for her to work for them. She was close to completing her doctoral thesis on compounds stimulating feeding behavior in cats. This was tricky work as many felines were notoriously finicky. She spent fifteen-hour days almost seven days a week to complete her project. The convention was a way for her to get ideas and potentially find a future employer when she finished her commitment to AGWorld.

It was on this wandering through posters and booths she found Dr. Mohr's lecture--"How We Became Fat." The venue on the edge of the convention hall was a small room meant to hold fifty people but there were about seventy people occupying the space. The audience was mainly men in their early fifties. Some wore suits but many only wore collared shirts. She squeezed herself into the small lecture hall and found a small space by the LCD projector to stand. Charles had noticed the stark contrast of an attractive woman among the middle-aged men and stumbled a little bit when he saw her.

The focus of the talk was a newly described hormone called leptin that was produced in fat cells and decreased appetite. Theoretically if a person had more leptin they would be less hungry and vice versa. Charles showed a diagram of leptin going from the fat to the brainstem.

"So how do we decrease leptin?" a man with a Texas accent interrupted.

"Why would anyone want to decrease leptin?" Charles replied, puzzled.

"You are at a food convention, Doctor. I think you can figure it out," the man replied.

The whole audience began to laugh. Daria looked around and smiled for a second. She thought that it was a pretty cruel assault but was awkwardly trying to fit in with the old boys' club. *This poor, smart, handsome man was being discredited by these unscientific market-driven jerks.*

"Currently, there is no way to lower leptin. Its physiology is not that well-known. What research is being done is focused on raising levels of leptin and making it more effective to reduce obesity," Charles responded.

This displeased much of the audience. Many of the men grumbled and left the small room. Daria took the opportunity to grab a seat and rest her feet that had been tortured by the high heels she wore. She continued to listen to his talk, trying to digest the biochemistry of appetite. Charles moved then to the marketing of food to small children. This discussion diminished the remaining audience, leaving a handful of curious scientists. When he finished his talk and answered questions from the podium, he waited to answer any further questions by the door of the conference room.

Daria was the only person that walked up to him afterwards. One of the men that Daria passed had his bald head bent backwards snoring away. Charles was twitching nervously as she approached. When she saw his face close up, his forehead beaded with sweat.

"Dr. Mohr, hi, Daria Eleutherios. I'm studying feeding behavior in cats at Rutgers." Daria stuck out her hand.

"Great! You made it through the entire talk. I'm afraid I really bored people." Charles wiped his sweaty palm on his pants and shook her hand.

"I think you're just focused on the opposite research to what these guys want to hear. I did want to ask if what you described in mice and in humans can be applied to cats," Daria comforted him, genuinely interested in his answer.

Daria and Dr. Mohr spent several minutes talking shop. Dr. Mohr's formal talk had ended at five-thirty, and at six-fifteen they were still standing at the door outside the conference center. Right before Daria was going to ask if they could have dinner and talk some more, a large, pale man in a grey suit interrupted them.

"Hi, Dr. Mohr, Sheldon Hairston, AGWorld taste ingredients research and development." Hairston shook Dr. Mohr's hand. He then took hold of Daria's upper arm with his left hand. "Daria has been missing from a very important R & D meeting; sorry for the interruption," Hairston hissed as he pulled her away from him.

Dr. Mohr was stunned and watched as she was escorted away. She had just said she was at Rutgers. *What would this corporate thug want with her?*

"Dr. Mohr--maybe we can talk about this later," she turned to him and gave him her business card.

Hairston and Daria walked briskly down the hall. Dr. Mohr looked down at her business card that read: Rutgers-AGWorld Cooperative Scientist.

"We can't have you giving corporate secrets to this guy," Hairston growled, grabbing her arm more tightly. His voice was a tense whisper to make sure Dr. Mohr didn't hear them.

"Ow. What are you talking about? We were just talking science and I think he's kind of cute," Daria fired back. She shook her arm, freeing herself from Hairston's claw.

"We don't need to add fuel to his fire. He already thinks there is some corporate agenda in making people fat. Just cool it. Read some of his reviews in the journals. Fawn over his picture in the conference program, but you don't actually have to speak to the guy. Now let's get dinner with some of the other co-op folks," Hairston ordered.

"Yes, Father," Daria said sarcastically.

Later that evening after dinner, Daria walked into the hotel bar and found Dr. Mohr hunched over a vodka and tonic. He was the only person sitting at the bar. A few corporate managers were standing in the room with their neckties loosened and smoking cigars. The burned tobacco was making her a little nauseous but she was happy to see Dr. Mohr again.

"Drinking your troubles away," Daria smiled at Dr. Mohr.

"My friend from Rutgers, what are you drinking?" Dr. Mohr asked with slightly slurred speech. He didn't want to even broach the subject of what happened with the Hairston guy.

"I'll just have a vodka and cranberry juice, thanks," Daria said between the bartender and Dr. Mohr. "Are you sober enough to go back to talking shop?" Daria asked and smiled again, estimating Dr. Mohr's degree of inebriation.

Dr. Mohr stopped drinking and they continued their conversation on obesity. It slowly delved into where each other lived, favorite musicians, and best date. Daria flicked her long blonde-brown hair playfully. Dr. Mohr was comfortable enough with her to start touching her shoulder. He insisted that she call him Charles. The bar lights then started to dim.

"Well, I better get going, the bar's about to close," Daria said.

"Aww, and I was having such a good time," Charles replied.

"Our offices are so close. We should get together when we are both on the East Coast," Daria suggested. She gave him a hug and kissed him on the cheek.

Dr. Mohr watched her thin body move in her skirt suit. It had been an interesting and very enjoyable encounter.

Daria was called by Hairston a week later. He had re-thought about her spending more time with Dr. Mohr. This for one of two reasons: to find out more about how specifically he connects the food industry to obesity and also to find out how the food industry can use hormones he spoke about to enhance the consumer's intake. He only mentioned to her the second reason, as this fell in line with her research and wouldn't seem to her to be too much like spying. He told her that she would get a large bonus for this extra activity. The tasks seemed simple enough to her and allowed her to learn more for her own research, make some extra money, and spend time with a smart, attractive man.

Chapter 6

"I had my reasons."

They drove to the outskirts of the city. The area was as bleak as Willie's neighborhood. Jason was still not used to traveling in such ravaged neighborhoods. *Where is Willie taking me? Who is this great person that we are going to meet?* The people he wanted answers from were in board rooms and palatial mansions. Willie was going to be the Tonto in his Lone Ranger crusade. He at least did not need to worry about his car being stolen. The blue, rust-speckled Toyota Corolla attracted minimal attention. His first book had netted him some large profits but he wanted to keep his Bohemian roots, although he secretly kept a second Ellicott City home with a garage filled with a BMW and large SUV.

"Pull in here," Willie said and pointed.

"What in here?" Jason questioned nervously. It was ten o'clock in the morning but where he was pulling his car in was still scary.

"Yeah man, she's in here," Willie smiled at Jason.

They both got out of the car. The air smelled of oil and gasoline fumes. It was a partly cloudy day and the sun was darting in and out. They walked along a dirt path by the side of a ten-foot-tall rusting red corrugated steel fence. It looked like it had been torn from the roof of a poor man's shack in India. In the distance they could hear multiple dogs barking. A plaque on one of the steel sheets read Bud's Junk and Auto Parts.

Jason wondered if he was going to meet the great, all-knowing Colonel Kurtz from *Apocalypse Now*. In the midst of all the horror he would get to meet a visionary. Amongst the savage natives, he would find the crux of knowledge that would bear fruit for his book.

"Hey, Willie, long time no see," bellowed a heavyset man with a garbled voice. He was sitting on a metal-framed lawn chair with a beer can in his right hand. He wore a white t-shirt with multiple grease stains and what looked like blood. He also wore a green John Deere baseball cap whose bill was flipped backward.

"Jon, how are you? Long time no see. How's Bud doing?" Willie shook his hand.

"Bud's been dead for 'bout a year," Jon said and spit chewing tobacco on the mud next to the chair rail.

"Sorry to hear. How's my girl? You been keeping her safe?" Willie asked changing his expression from a frown to a smile after mentioning his girl.

"Yeah, kept it safe. I can't unload her after all these years. Nobody wants that piece of shit," Jon chuckled to himself, nearly choking on his spit.

"I just wanted to see how she was doing," Willie grumbled.

"This ain't a storage facility. We own her and if you take anything out of her it's ours. Hey, Willie who is your girlfriend?"

"This is Jason. He's a writer. We are checking out the old girl for a story," Willie explained. Willie was being very cautious around this poor white man, a reflex he believed harkened back to the time African-Americans served poor, white slave masters. In the junkyard here it felt like times had changed little since those pre-Civil War days.

"Pleased to meet you," Jason stuck out his hand.

Jon disregarded Jason's hand. If there was one thing poor people of any ethnicity distrusted, it was intellectual elite people. Jon got rid of the rest of the dip in his mouth and drank a swig of his beer. He stood up and nodded to a person at the gate. "Luke, let Willie and his writer pal in for a peek. Willie, she's on row seventeen."

"We'll be out in a little bit," Willie said.

Despite the clouds breaking up, Jason and Willie walked progressively in darkness as they moved through paths whose walls were made of cars piled up twenty feet high. The sound of dogs was getting closer to them. Many of the cars they passed by were crushed. Some of the aisles had shelves filled with auto parts.

After passing aisles seven through twelve, they found the barking dogs; three Rottweilers with heavy-gauge chains around there necks anchored to a common large post in the ground. All three of them lunged at them with saliva dripping from their mouths.

"You three shut the hell up," an older, thin man snarled from the seat of a forklift.

"Thank you, we were just looking for number seventeen," Willie said.

"Can't y'all read? The sign says 'beware of dog.' Heh, heh. Seventeen is down there behind aisle thirteen." The man smacked his gums due to his lack of teeth. The forklift kicked up dust as the man drove by them.

"We're here. There she is," Willie announced, smiling.

"Who? What? This thing?" Jason lifted his hands.

"It's a 1973 Grumman delivery truck. It's a beaut'. Don't you think?" Willie opened his palms as if he was at a car show displaying the latest futuristic model.

"It's a box on wheels, Willie. And what is this 'Neptune' written on the side?" Jason was puzzled why they were looking at this ugly vehicle. The truck was a gunmetal grey rectangle with a little trapezoidal snout. The tires had been removed as well as much of the shiny trim and reflectors. On the side of the truck just above a swing-down door was a sign in blue and red lettering that read "Neptune's Sandwiches and Hot Dogs."

"There is a lot of history in here, young writer. This is a time machine of Orwellian proportions. Just get inside and take a ride." Willie's eyes widened and his teeth glistened as he slid the passenger door backward.

"I'd rather not," Jason said and crossed his arms.

"A young man with big dreams used to drive this old girl to the Baltimore loading docks. I had a nice, new Lincoln and a lot of money in my pocket. I had a future back then. I was going to finish studying economics, get my MBA, and rise with the biotech industry," Willie reminisced, dazed with memories of the past.

"What happened to those dreams, Willie?" Jason asked and raised his right eyebrow.

"That's a story for another day. Back in the seventies, this was a summer job that was going to help me pay for business school and pay for my grandmother's surgery," Willie replied. He wanted to focus on the feeling of promise and not dwell on failure.

"Wait. I don't understand this. A sandwich truck to pay for your grandmother's surgery? Hello? What's the connection Willie?!" Jason yelled as he was getting many more questions than answers for his book. He wondered how any of this connected the food industry and obesity.

Willie sat on the peeling blue vinyl seat and began to tell the story. "When I was working at the Stevenson lab, Dr. Stevenson gave me an idea of how I could pay for my MBA. Before I get into that, let me enlighten you as to how I came to know Dr. Stevenson. I thought I was a visionary. I had studied how regular people, meaning non-celebrities, made money. I read the *Wall Street Journal* and came to the conclusion that biotechnology would be the wave of the future. I was going to earn my business degree but I thought I should at least find out what it's like to be in a biology lab. I answered an ad in a student newspaper for a lab tech, which was essentially a dishwasher and mouse feeder. This was how I began at Joe Stevenson's lab," Willie explained, waving his arms as he told the story.

"And he suggested that you start a food truck that would pay for your Master's degree and surgery for you grandmother?" Jason asked cynically.

"My grandmother had a bad heart valve. She couldn't move without being short of breath. She was heavy, and to compound this, her legs were twice their original size. She needed surgery soon but we didn't have the insurance to cover the surgery. So Dr. Stevenson told me to buy a lunch truck. With a grant from AG-USA, he would see to it that my grandmother got her surgery and that I would get my MBA." Willie nodded, concurring with his own story.

"You're a smart man, Willie. What was the catch?" Jason asked skeptically.

"I knew they paid you those big journalism bucks for something. Now come inside and I'll show you." Willie waved him into the van.

"Uh…" Jason hesitated.

"You won't know if you stay out there," Willie said as he proceeded to the back of the van.

Jason followed and stepped inside. It listed a little bit to the side when he entered. He grabbed the dashboard with his right hand and with his left he grabbed the doorway. The only light inside came from two square, blue glass vent windows on the roof and the front windshield that had multiple spider web cracks. Inside it smelled of decaying leaves and in one corner there was something that looked like a burrow or nest. Jason peered around, feeling the cobwebs on his cheek. He saw Willie in the middle of the rear cabin with his hand on his chin moving himself in a circle looking at the ground.

"I know it's here somewhere." Willie stared at different areas of the mangy grey-green carpet of the van floor.

"What are you looking for? Maybe we should ask for a flashlight," Jason suggested.

"Yeah, do you want to ask the extras from *Deliverance* for a flashlight? Be my guest. Oh, there it is," Willie clucked and crouched down on the floor by the nest of leaves. He felt for a hole in the carpet and when he found it he tore a ten-inch-by-ten-inch chunk of rug out. He then lifted the lid off a little compartment. When he stood up and turned to Jason, he held up three test tubes. Two of the tubes were a golden color, the other was black. Willie tipped them from side to side to show Jason their oily viscosity.

"What's that?" Jason looked at him puzzlingly.

"This is the reason for the extra money. It's also the reason why you came to me. This one's seal is broken and is probably bad but the other two are probably as good as when they came from the lab," Willie asserted. He brought the tubes closer to Jason and pointed to the individual tubes.

"That's an additive?" Jason asked.

"The first generation, and probably the best food enhancer there ever was. Jason, I was the observer in a study. I went to the docks and the longshoremen would come to my truck. I put a little bit of it on sandwiches and hot dogs and gave them to certain customers and watched how many times they came back. The guys who ate the additive returned more often than those who didn't eat it. Dr. Stevenson wanted regular updates and would call me at a local watering hole I frequented. I also wrote all of this in a journal. When I presented my data to Dr. Stevenson, he said I was a real scientist. He then told me to give *all* the workers the additive. The workers who initially did not receive the additive now started coming more frequently to my truck. It started to get very confusing because several of the workers were sending their friends to pick up food and they would rotate with breaks. Overall, it seemed to be a good experiment that proved that this stuff was a damn good food additive," Willie said and lifted the tubes.

"You know, you probably should have informed the longshoremen," Jason remarked.

"You're probably right. We did this a few years after the Tuskegee story broke but when I voiced my concerns to Dr. Stevenson, he told me the government agencies said it was okay and that this was more of a marketing study," Willie countered defensively and started out of the van.

"You know, I can't put my finger on it, but this experiment wasn't altogether harmless. I need to show you something in my car," Jason said.

"Well, whatever it was, I was a naive pawn in the world of science. I had my reasons," Willie declared loudly. He didn't want to think he did anything wrong, though his gut ached over it.

"Willie, what happened to your MBA and grandmother?" Jason asked to lead the conversation away from what appeared to have aggravated Willie.

"Get the fug out the way!" The man on the forklift had come to aisle seventeen and stopped his machine suddenly. Willie and Jason put their backs against the van. The forklift sped along the path.

"I'd rather not talk about that now as it doesn't concern your book," Willie said with a grumble. He started walking down the path toward the gate.

"Then who the heck is Neptune? Did you operate a fish truck?" Jason asked.

"No, no. That was my nickname. I was a Division I champion high school freestyle and breaststroke swimmer. The swimming got me a partial college scholarship. It also helped me one day when I was at the docks. Some big fellow had fallen in the water and was a horrible swimmer. A rip tide was carrying him out into open water. Several other guys had tried to throw life preservers and jump in but no one had reached him. When I heard this, I ran to the docks and dived in. By the time I got to him, he had swallowed a lot of the grease-laden water. We made it safely back to a ladder where I helped him up. I like to sometimes think that after this episode, I increased the food truck business. But that probably wasn't the case." Willie smiled at the memory of his lost youth.

They had reached the gate of the junk yard. The youth behind the counter looked like he'd just left high school. He had a lot of acne, wore a black Misfits t-shirt and a spiked wristband. His maroon baseball hat was turned backwards and covered his greasy blond hair.

"Just these," Willie said and presented the tubes to the young man.

"Jon, what's the price on three tubes of yellow stuff?" the youth asked.

"Aw, fuck! Luke, you're gonna have to be a little bit more descriptive." Jon sat up from his lawn chair. His face was red and he looked visibly angry for having to break with his momentum. His cheek bulged with a fresh wad of chew. He bent his back a little and squinted at the objects in Willie's hand.

"Shit, Willie! Can't you just buy a crankshaft or radiator or something? I gotta make ends meet here. Take your piss water and get outta here." Jon waved his hand at them and sat back down in his lawn chair.

"Thanks Jon," Willie muttered.

Luke opened the gate for them. They both got into the Corolla. Jason opened the glove box and Willie carefully placed all three tubes in amongst the random paper and trash.

"So what is it that you wanted to show me?" Willie grudgingly asked.

Jason reached backward from the driver's seat into the back passenger foot well and pulled out a brown accordion folder. He undid the string and rifled through papers that did not seem to have any particular organization.

"Ah, here it is," Jason perkily exclaimed.

"What is it?"

"This is a scatter plot of disability claims due to heart disease at the Baltimore docks. There was a spike here around five years after you left," Jason explained, pointing to the X and Y axes of the graph.

"You don't know longshoremen. They're a pretty unhealthy lot. They smoke and they drink. That doesn't prove anything," Willie scoffed.

"On this graph is an overlay of the men who were also obese. It was an exact match."

Jason showed Willie another plot of obesity and heart disease in the longshoremen.

"Yeah, and those guys were not obese before meeting me? You really don't have anything. I stopped selling food five years before these claims were made. Are you saying that the additive turns on the appetite forever?" Willie asked doubtfully. He was trying to make a point to Jason that the association of food additive could not be the sole cause of their maladies.

"Maybe. Maybe it kicked something off in their bodies that would make them eat more. The additive might have entered the general food supply and these unlucky guys just got a head start," Jason explained.

"Too speculative," Willie said and turned to the passenger side window.

"When we talk to your former boss, we might get the answer to these questions," Jason replied confidently.

"Nobody's seen him in years," Willie replied.

"Is your passport up to date? How about a trip to Lucerne?" Jason smiled at Willie.

"Switzerland?" Willie furrowed his brow in a what-the-hell-are-you-talking-about manner.

Jason started the Corolla.

*   *   *

A black Crown Victoria was parked across the street next to a competing junk yard. Inside were two men. One of the men was using binoculars to look at Jason and Willie in the Corolla.

"What'd'ya think they're saying, 'a Whopper is better than a Big Mac?'" the man in a wrinkled white collared shirt and grey blazer asked.

"Tony, I can't believe they crammed us in a car together to do surveillance. We are a true odd couple. Where was it that they dug you up?" an

African-American man asked from behind the wheel. He wore wire-rimmed glasses and his dark suit fit his toned body well.

"The FBI. I worked on mob cases. Where were you again, 'lijah? In the accounting office bean-counting?" Tony joked and jammed a sausage bagel into his mouth, getting sauce on his shirt.

"No, not at all. I did criminal investigation with the Secret Service, counterfeiting," Elijah said, shaking his head.

"So, I was told we needed to stake these guys out. One guy is a writer and the other is a newspaper salesman. What are we investigating, a conflict-of-interest crime here? Payola at the newspaper shack? This is ridiculous," Tony scoffed and turned away from Elijah.

"Jason wants to write about food and obesity. The other guy, Willie--also known as Neptune--is a source for him. They may discover unsightly information that could throw off the coming presidential election. You must have read some of the briefing?" Elijah asked and raised his eyebrows.

"Yeah, I skimmed it. I don't know why we are chasing this writer guy and the god of war. Are they trying to find the next Gary Hart? We should be finding the next terror cell. I guess it's just our tax dollars at work to keep us in Gucci loafers," Tony said sarcastically and began to suck on his teeth.

"The god of the sea, you mean. Just keep an eye on those two and help me navigate," Elijah spat, annoyed.

Tony grabbed the binoculars. The red Corolla slowly pulled out of the junk yard and headed back to downtown Washington. Elijah gently tapped the accelerator and kept a safe distance from their target.

Chapter 7

"Mmmm, fruity."

Gordon Irving took a puff of his cigar and laid it in an old glass U.S. Air force ashtray. He leaned back in his brown leather chair and his eyes darted back and forth at a television monitor broadcasting various poll numbers and a computer screen flashing a stock ticker of all the major U.S, Asian and European markets. He took another puff of his cigar and buzzed his personal assistant.

"Mr. Irving, I have the progress so far from the agents," Marc Olesson said as he walked in. He wore a navy blazer with a dark purple shirt and a tie with multiple stripes. With his tall, thin frame and Scandinavian looks, he stood out like a model compared to his blandly dressed colleagues.

"And what do they say?" Mr. Irving asked eagerly.

"They have found a Mr. Willie Barnes talking to the journalist. They went to a junkyard."

"What did they find at the junkyard?"

"They didn't say."

"This isn't good." Mr. Irving paused. His face turned red with rage and his eyes squinted. The wrinkles of his sixty-something-year-old face had deeper crevices. His left hand squeezed the armrest of his chair and he leaned forward. He inhaled deeply on his cigar and exhaled in Marc's direction.

"Mr. Irving, sir, Mr. Golberg said that his surveillance team was good and they believed it was some kind of fact-finding mission. They didn't think anything of importance would come of it. At least there was nothing they were going to find that they couldn't find out when they searched the writer's apartment," Marc offered and held his breath. Sweat formed on his brow. He was glad he'd used a generous amount of apple cinnamon cologne to cut the stench of the cigar smoke.

"I would have liked a precision job. Looks like Goldberg's gotten a couple of clowns to do the work. The future Mr. President will soon decide who will be his vice president, and I want to keep all skeletons buried. I would like to keep my agrarian, hillbilly, NASCAR-dad image intact. That is to say--a man of the people, not a corporate tyrant. This journalist can make me stink, and the party chairman can smell a stink on the East Coast when he's on the West. These boys that Goldberg has need to be precise. I look out for those who look out for me, so it's in *your* interests to win also. Besides, a vice president's chief of staff position looks pretty good on the resume," Mr. Irving mused and gave Marc a one-sided smile. He paused, his face starting to redden again.

Marc awaited a new outburst but wondered how contrary to this image Mr. Irving actually was. Mr. Irving was a second-generation attorney who grew up in a wealthy suburb of Washington. His father had inherited his grandfather George Irving's steel company. George had been the navigator of the family and had witnessed the decline in the U.S. steel industry. He sold his interests in the company so that his son could be involved in the food industry, an industry that showed no limits. The younger Irvings received their law degrees to prove to their fathers that they were not dullards. As a previous board member and then chief executive of AG-USA, now AGWorld, he courted both political parties to achieve more profits for his company. To Marc, the middle-aged man in front of him was still a go-getter and a cutthroat master of industry who could smile one minute and wreak havoc the next.

"I don't know what this idealistic writer wants with me. Maybe he thinks I made poor people poorer. Maybe I even made them fatter. The speculation is all out there. How did this old white guy from a privileged background fuck over the common man? Did he ever think maybe the common man fucked himself? The common man is a common man not because of lack of opportunity or the hurdles placed by *uncommon* men, but because he cannot genetically do it. It is evolutionary so," Mr. Irving proclaimed, rocking back and forth in his chair while creating a tent with his fingers.

"Evolution, sir?" Marc asked, to placate his boss.

"Yes, evolution, Marc. There was an economic theorist in the late 1700s who espoused the theory that poverty or the poor can be decreased in number by the amount of misery placed upon them." Irving's facial color softened to a pale white as he recanted his theories.

"Is that the theory of life according to Thomas Malthus?" Marc asked, like a good pupil.

"Ah, Marc, you *are* actually listening to me. You've got that VP chief of staff position locked in. Malthus' theory on poverty included the idea that misery— at his time, famine—would keep overpopulation in check. In our case, it may be an *increase* in food that quells a population surge. Why not make a little money off of that? Especially if it gives the poor nothing but pleasure to eat. What throws off the advantage for the uncommon man is the handout. Do you know that in this country, wealth makes you more likely to exercise? It is the uncommon man who figures out one's environment--this is where Darwin comes in. If you cannot get to the point where you know the environment is hurting you, it must be the genetics of how your brain is wired that's preventing the understanding. These people lack the understanding that advantage comes from *here* and not *here*." Mr. Irving pointed to his head and then grabbed Marc by the bicep.

Marc looked down at the arm grabbing him. "Could it be that the rich just have more leisure time to pursue exercise and have more education in nutrition?"

"Many of the masses don't even come close to the concept. The reason they do not have the time or the education is because of the professions they were pre-destined to be a part of. You might even call it a Calvinistic professional calling. Again, they are victims of their genetics because the environment has beaten them. You and I are uncommon men; we evolved to beat the system,"

Mr. Irving said and smiled. He grabbed a picture on his desk and stared at the image of his striking blonde daughter taken ten years ago.

"But what of the great men who have had scandals happen to them? Do you think that they evolved into the scandals?" Marc asked meekly to challenge his teacher.

"Life is always a game of chance. Did the T-Rex see the meteor coming? Evolution is a game of likelihood. What are the chances that a third grader can read at an eighth grade level? Small, but it could happen. These small differences are what you would call the mutations. But bad things happen, like to my uncle over there on the wall." Irving pointed to a painting of his uncle heroically looking out to sea on an aircraft carrier in front of his Wildcat fighter jet. "He was a great man, as great as my father, but he was killed by a kamikaze Japanese pilot in World War II; a victim of chance."

"I don't think that the theory is complete. What about people with glasses?" Marc interrupted. "Shouldn't they have died out years ago? They wouldn't have been able to find their food in prehistoric times."

Mr. Irving chuckled under his breath. "Well, people needing glasses must have had some value back then. There are quite a few intelligent people who need glasses. There may be some holes in the theory, but they are small. We could really come out big if we think methodically. This would be a big step for me--and for you as well. We can keep the machinery going. My family will be set for many generations. The economic advantages of an executive are great. The agencies controlled by the executive are numerous from the environment, the military, education, and health. You can find a contract from the government to make money. All the while, you can be seen as a statesman and man of the people." Mr. Irving looked above Marc at the far wall of the office.

"Well hopefully we help people when we are in the higher echelons of government," Marc replied.

"The uncommon men will not be disappointed. There are holes, Marc. Definitely, holes in the theory. Hmmm." Mr. Irving took a deep, nasal breath. "Mmmm, fruity. Many of these holes, I do not understand." He gave Marc a devilish smile. Mr. Irving thought it was time to end his conversation with Marc. He had no confirmation if Marc was homosexual but liked to hint at it as a way of letting Marc know he was keeping him in check. Mr. Irving wrote a small note on a pad on his desk, folded it, and placed it in an envelope. He crouched down, put his right hand on Marc's shoulder, and whispered to him. "Give this to Goldberg personally and don't open it. And on a different topic, it would be nice if my personal assistant had a wife." Mr. Irving squeezed Marc's shoulder and turned to sit back at his desk.

"I'll get this to him right away. But on the other matter—" Marc stopped mid-sentence as Mr. Irving had stuck up his hand to motion him out of the office as he began to talk on the phone. Marc hated people prying into his personal affairs. He didn't want his boss's views foisted on him. He did his work and did it well despite having an ogre of a boss. He hated feeling that something was wrong with him. Who did this guy think he was? Marc closed the office door as the anger compounded inside of him.

*　　*　　*

After Marc left, Irving thought about his chances of becoming vice president. He stared at an old pocket watch his father had given him. His forefinger and thumb twirled the chain so that it spun. In this yet undecided election, he had worked his way into the campaigns of the top three candidates of his party. The candidates and the campaign managers generally liked him and no matter what spectrum of the politics in the party, liberal or conservative, they thought he would be a good fit. Vice president these days was usually reserved for an elected governor or congressman. He would be the second unelected official and Secretary of Agriculture to be appointed vice president since FDR chose Henry Wallace for his 1940 campaign. Irving was seen by the candidates to be a natural leader and business-savvy as CEO of AG World--good for the business vote. As Secretary of Agriculture, he championed the end of hunger in the US, proper alternatives for school lunches, and hunger aid to foreign nations, all of which made him a favorite of the everyman. These humanitarian causes did have a catch, in that the policies were tailored to financially benefit AG World. He still had plenty of stock in the company through shadow investments that were not publicly known or declared. As this election season approached, he believed his resume positioned him well to become the next Vice President. Then maybe after four years he'd become president. He smiled at the thought of his father seeing him from the afterlife as vice president or president. He relished the thought of the near unlimited worldly powers. In a moment, he grabbed the twisting pocket watch and thought about the men disclosing to the public his role in the widespread use of an appetite-enhancing food additive. That food additive helped Irving turn a regional agricultural firm into a worldwide conglomerate and got him this far in public office. Ironically, the additive may *prevent* him from attaining higher office. He disliked the way he would be perceived by the papers when any one of the men who gave them the information were also involved with initial studies and were technically culpable. *They would get off scot-free when they incriminated him. They had nothing to lose but he had everything to.* He squeezed the watch to the point where he nearly broke the crystal. Irving ran through the options and all he could think of is getting rid of the mouthpiece, the person who could put the pieces together and connect him to the food additive: the journalist. *The other men separately were not credible: the newspaperman--not believable; the doctor--can't connect the dots when he was a teenager in the lab; Stevenson--might be a problem if his mental health suddenly improves, but unlikely.* He loosened his grip on the watch and leaned back in his chair, feeling slightly more relieved after mulling his options.

Chapter 8

"Willie, don't mortgage your future on the past."

Jason and Willie boarded the Swiss Air Airbus and sat down next to each other. The plane was somewhat crowded, with scant overhead storage room. They watched as people lined the aisle waiting to sit down as others hunted and pecked to find a place for their overhead bags. The strange and coarse Brooklyn accent of an unkempt, suit-wearing, obese man caught their ears. He seemed to be complaining about the size of the plane to his African-American colleague.

"First class--I have never traveled this way. Maybe I should take up writing. Those poor folks in coach," Willie remarked and chuckled to himself.

"Well, the publisher likes the story and likes me too. So that helps to get these tickets. When I told them I needed to get some key elements in the story down with my key piece of evidence--you--they told me they would book the tickets," Jason said and smiled. He anticipated this was going to be a big book, bigger than his first.

"Thank you," Willie muttered to the stewardess who poured him a glass of liquor.

"Willie, in order to make sure I have the correct context for your responses, it might be good for me to understand why a man with such promise ended up running a newspaper stand in that war zone in Washington, DC," Jason stated. He wanted to know more about this fellow that he liked. He wished to understand the backstory and personalities behind the big picture of food additives and obesity.

"It's a hard story to tell," Willie began as he reclined in the leather chair. He took a swig of the glass of Jack Daniel's left by the stewardess, and recited the story.

* * *

The sun shone bright on the block in Washington where Willie and his grandmother lived. Mrs. Barnes sat on her porch watching the large vehicles pass by. About half a block down the street, one of her neighbor's houses had burned down. The residual smoke blended with the morning dew and irritated her throat. She hacked up some white phlegm with blood streaks and spat it out in the small plot of grass in front of the porch. She heard a rumble from inside the house.

Willie ran down the stairs and opened the creaky screen door.

"Grandma, what's for break—" Willie stopped short. "Are you okay? You shouldn't be out here with all this smoke."

Mrs. Barnes waved at him with a white tissue clutched in her hand and coughed some more. "Don't you worry about me, William. I see you're about ready to go to work, my grandbaby. You go on inside and eat some breakfast."

Willie looked at his grandmother, who was intermittently coughing and spitting. Her legs were very big. She wore slippers on her feet as she could no longer fit into shoes. He knew that she was old and she would eventually pass away. She was only in her mid-sixties and before her heart attack a few years ago she'd been his pillar of strength. She resisted many of Willie's attempts to help her as she insisted that she was self-sufficient. He looked down at his bell-bottom jeans and dusted them off.

"I can wash them when you get back. You don't want your co-workers saying you come from a dirty poor house. Now eat something before you go." She smiled with pride at Willie.

"What do we have?" Willie was anxious to leave.

"I made some grits and some bacon," Mrs. Stevens answered as she watched a crane arrive to tear down the charred remains of the row home.

"Ugh, Grandma, you know I don't like grits. I'll just have some Fruit Loops and a couple of pieces of bacon." Willie opened the screen door and turned, looking first at his grandmother's edematous legs and then at her face. "Are you going to Dr. Thomas's today?"

"Don't worry about me. It's at two and the Deacon from the church is going to drive me," she yelled but stayed fixated on the action across the street, as the wood of the demolished house crumpled and cracked under the weight of the crane.

Willie closed the door behind him. The inside of the house was filled with Victorian furniture with tables covered with crocheted doilies. The walls were filled with memories of Willie's parents, his father's college diploma, a teenage picture of his mother in the church choir, a photo of the two of them and young William in front of the family's first car. Other pictures filled the room, including a picture of Dr. King at his grandmother's church and a picture of her late Cocker spaniel. He walked on a worn red and green rug into the small kitchen. He grabbed the box of Fruit Loops from on top of the fridge and shoved a handful into his mouth. There were four pieces of bacon on a paper napkin and he took a couple together and started chewing on them. Willie looked out at the backyard where the grass was just starting to poke through after the winter freeze. Behind a chain link fence, there was junk piled almost five feet high. This angered Willie, as he and his grandmother tried their hardest to make their neighborhood a great place but there was always a seemingly defiant neighbor. Willie gobbled his food down and took a swig of orange juice from the carton in the fridge and looked at his watch. He realized he was running late and quickly left the house. He opened the screen door and kissed his grandmother on her forehead.

"Bye baby, be good," Mrs. Barnes said and smiled at Willie.

"You too," Willie replied. He walked down the stairs to the walkway and picked up some trash. He threw it in the garbage can and continued several blocks to the bus station. On the bus ride he reflected about how he had already come this far in life. He had worked at Stevenson's lab for about six months. Dr. Stevenson was very friendly and intelligent. It was still early dawn after the civil rights movement, but Joe Stevenson treated Willie as an equal, as if society had already fully integrated. The two of them would often go for drinks late at night after working in the lab. If Willie had had a great desire to study biology, he would have wanted Dr. Stevenson to be his mentor.

One night when drinking at a local college tavern, Dr. Stevenson presented Willie with an idea about how he could make some extra money. The bar was dark, loud and thick with tobacco smoke. College students were playing darts in the corner and singing along to The Who's *Magic Bus*. Dr, Stevenson's straight, graying brown hair was falling in his face and he kept trying to get it out of his eyes by blowing air up at it or moving it with his hand. The bartender brought them two Jack Daniel's and Dr. Pepper.

"Cheers to another semester down," Dr. Stevenson smiled.

"Here, here," Willie agreed.

He and Stevenson drank a hearty gulp.

"Willie, I wish you would reconsider this degree in finance nonsense," Dr. Stevenson said.

"Your work is interesting, sir, but my desire is to make a lot of money. I think I have the same knack for business as my parents did," Willie argued.

"All right, Willie, I'm disappointed I can't precept you as a scientist. One of the reasons I wanted to meet with you is that I have an idea that can make you a bit of money. This may aid in achieving some your financial dreams." Stevenson smiled.

"Well, you have got my full attention." Willie tilted his ear toward Stevenson as if words would pass easier into his brain if he did so.

"I want to get you out of the drudgery of tech work and into some research. I can't tell you too much right now. The company that is sponsoring the research is willing to pay top dollar to get results. You would be paid fairly handsomely for your help in the project." Dr. Stevenson looked him in the eye and put a hand on his shoulder.

"Why me? There are post-docs and pre-med students that would love a chance to work on a well-funded research project. What about Charlie?" Willie countered in disbelief.

"Charlie and the others are not people-persons. They relate well to the rodents but the research the company wants to do is human. The study is harmless, Willie. Besides, despite the fact I have known you for a short period of time, I can trust you," Dr. Stevenson replied and took another swig of his drink.

"This sounds hard for me to believe. What do I have to do? How much will I be paid? " Willie asked. He gave Dr. Stevenson a worried look.

"Willie, Willie, come on now. This is all on the up-and-up. The company hasn't given me the design yet but they assured me that it passes all regulations for human study. You're in finance. This is going to be more like a survey. Willie, I have full confidence in you. The salary may cover the cost of your tuition. They said that if I find the right person for the job I should give them an advance," Dr. Stevenson explained and bent down to grab something out of his worn leather shoulder bag. He gave the white envelope that he retrieved to Willie.

"Wow!" Willie exclaimed as he peered into the contents of the envelope. Willie had never seen a hundred dollar bill up close before and now he had ten of them in his hands. This was a lot of money at the time as the average yearly wage for an unskilled worker was only four thousand dollars.

"Willie, can I put my trust in you?" Dr. Stevenson asked and again reached out to put his hand on Willie's shoulder.

Willie was dazed. He looked at the money, felt it and counted it over and over again to make sure it was real. "I'll probably do it but I think I should know more about my duties."

"Good, Willie. You'll like the research. I'll let you keep the advance because I am confident you will be okay with this. Listen, I have to go home and tuck the wife and kids in. I will see you tomorrow and explain the details." Dr. Stevenson paid the bar tab and walked out.

Willie placed the envelope in the inside pocket of his jacket and walked out of the bar with crossed arms. He walked like that all the way home to prevent any loss of his windfall. The next morning he counted the money again and dashed out of the house. His early-twenties sensibilities had kicked in with the idea of spending for today and not worrying about tomorrow. So instead of letting his finance-tuned brain influence him, he walked not into the local stock broker's office but the local Lincoln dealer. The coupe was a leftover model from last year and Willie had more than enough cash for the down payment.

Willie sat behind the wheel of his Lincoln parked a few blocks from his house. He thought about the weeks that had gone by without hearing the details about his duties in the project. It had been two months since he got the advance. Dr. Stevenson did not want to talk about the project while there were other people in the lab so they decided to meet outside of work instead. Willie hoped it wasn't a scam as he didn't want to hurt anybody. Dr. Stevenson did not act any differently toward him since he gave him the advance. It seemed as far as Dr. Stevenson was concerned Willie was the same, consistent lab tech. Willie sighed with the possibility of disappointment and turned the key to his Lincoln. He headed to a diner on the outskirts of town where they had agreed to meet.

The diner looked like an Airstream trailer attached to the ground with permanent stairs. The sun shone off the polished aluminum façade. There were only four cars in the lot. Willie got out of his car and climbed the steps. He walked into the diner and saw the back of Dr. Stevenson's head. He was talking to a man in a black suit and white shirt. The air in the diner was filled with the aroma of greasy meals. The man Dr. Stevenson was talking to pointed to him and Dr. Stevenson turned around and smiled at Willie. Willie walked up to the men.

"Willie! You made it. This is Alvin Huberty; he works for the company that's sponsoring the project," Dr. Stevenson said excitedly.

Alvin stood up, stuck his hand out, and smiled. Willie shook his hand and looked at the tobacco stained, crooked teeth of the abnormally pale man.

"Grab a seat and we can talk turkey. Speaking of which, do you want something to eat?" Stevenson asked.

"I'm not too hungry." Willie smiled nervously. He grabbed a wooden chair from a nearby table, not noticing that there was an obese man in a denim jumper and brown baseball hat sitting at the table. The obese man grumbled under his breath as if Willie had invaded his territory. Willie was oblivious and sat at the booth with Alvin and Dr. Stevenson. He was very nervous. This was his first business meeting. If he played his cards right, he would make a lot of money. He thought that maybe he might score a finance job with this research company.

"Willie, what we need you to do is observe people who eat a food additive," Dr. Stevenson said.

"OK, well that sounds pretty easy," Willie answered as he started to calm down. *Observing people sounded pretty benign.*

Alvin smiled. "Willie, what we're asking you to do is to put this additive in some food and give it to people. Then you write down their habits: note if they come back for more and how frequently. Dr. Stevenson tells me that you should go into biology because of your scientific powers of observation. We want you to look at these folks, befriend them, and find out if they enjoy the food and if they gain weight. We want you to do it in a casual manner in their own environment."

"I don't understand. So they are not in a research facility?" Willie asked. To Willie, this seemed a little like some of the sociology experiments that he read about in his 101 class where a strange element was introduced to the community and the sociologist observed reactions to it.

"Willie, this isn't an experiment. It's a survey, in the real world. Your work could affect millions of people. It's all on the up and up within all the regulations. Right, Alvin?" Dr. Stevenson motioned to Alvin to allay any of Willie's suspicions.

"Yes. It's all legal. But we don't want to blab or brag about this additive to anyone. Corporate spies are everywhere. Plus, we want our subjects to be blind. That is, we don't want them to be influenced by knowing if there is an additive or not," Alvin explained.

"I know what blinding is. This seems a little strange to me." Willie gave them a puzzled look and stared at the floor. He had begun to suspect it was really a drug trial. He knew there was a lot of regulations and subject consent required to do these studies. In other words, subjects had to know they were doing a drug trial.

Dr. Stevenson grabbed his upper arm and whispered, "Spies are everywhere. Even tubby over there could be a spy. This information needs to stay between the three of us." He pointed to the man in a brown hat. The man looked up and grunted as if in acknowledgement.

"We need you to get a food truck. The company will supply the additive and will give you the location of a food distributor. We will have you add a few drops of this to the different food items. Then we want to observe your patrons. It's that easy." Alvin lifted his hands as if he had just performed a magic trick.

"This still sounds like an experiment to me. I'm not very comfortable with this. What is the company?" Willie asked, trying to slow things down. It seemed like Mr. Huberty had assumed he was ready to go along with it.

"It's my company, Agricultural Technology, Inc. It's all regulated. Stevenson here has backed me up on this. We *did* give you an advance. It's pretty good money. But, if you don't want to participate we would like our money back," Alvin said without expression. Mr. Huberty had put up a fairly good front and added a layer between AG-USA, the true sponsor of the study and the additive.

Willie started to pull his chair out but Dr. Stevenson reached out and grabbed Willie's hand. "This is a great opportunity for you. You can pay off your student loans and pay for your final year of college. You have a lot of potential in biology or finance or whatever you do and this could get your foot in the door. Maybe Alvin here can even hook you up in the business world. Right, Alvin?"

"Yes, Willie. We would compensate you very well for your help. Pay for your tuition. This is how important your role would be." Alvin smiled again.

"Willie, I asked you because I have confidence in you. I have seen for the last six months that you are a hard, dedicated worker. Your hard work here will pay off in the end," Dr. Stevenson said.

Willie pushed his chair away from the table. "Dr. Stevenson, Mr. Huberty, I am going to have to think about this."

A woman in a blonde bouffant hairdo wearing a pink uniform with a white apron came up to the table. "Fellas, anything else I can getcha?"

Willie stood up without shaking hands and started to walk towards the exit.

Dr. Stevenson called out to him, "Sleep on it Willie. I have confidence in you."

Willie got into his car and drove toward his grandmother's house thinking about his present and his future. With the money they were offering he could even reopen his parents' shop. He could pay off all of his student loans. He could get a nurse for his grandmother. He could start looking for a serious girl-friend. It could be his ticket to a better life. But opposing these feelings of hope were ones of guilt and suspicion. These raced through his brain. *Why would they choose me? It doesn't seem like a study that needs "special skills." Couldn't they have hired somebody for this that wasn't already in the lab? Mr. Huberty says the study is approved and Dr. Stevenson must have looked into that. What is it that I don't know that I should know? How will I pay back the advance? Does the good that will happen to me if I accept this outweigh some of the bad that might happen? I wouldn't be using the money for evil purposes just helping myself and my family. Maybe this is God's attempt at making up for my parents' loss.*

A blaring horn sounded. Willie had just run through a red light and was nearly sideswiped by truck. He pulled over to a clear area of the street and took a couple of long deep breaths to clear his head. He was only a couple of blocks from his grandmother's house and he needed to concentrate on his driving and think briefly about a date he might have for next weekend.

Willie parked the car and walked up to his grandmother's porch. The sun was setting and a large swath of orange covered the horizon. Willie found more candy wrappers and beer cans on the sidewalk and he picked those up to put in the trash. His grandmother was sitting in the same chair with her head back, eyes closed and snoring. Dried tears stained her cheeks. Willie unfurled a blanked folded on her lap and placed it over her. Edna lifted her head and began to look around.

"Willie, my baby, how'd your meeting go?" Edna asked in a dry voice.

"Fine, I guess," Willie said softly.

"Willie, you look sad. Are you going to be okay? I need you to be strong, my baby," Edna insisted and smiled. She reached out to touch Willie's cheek and her eyes began to tear up.

"Grandma, what's wrong? How did things go with Dr. Thomas?" Willie asked with an anticipation of doom.

"He says my heart is weak, maybe too weak to go on for long. You see my swollen legs. That water is getting in my lungs, too. That heart attack I had a while back is catching up to me. He doesn't think I'll make it through the year," Edna whispered, tears pouring down her cheeks.

"What? No! Aw, Grandma. Isn't there something they can do? Medicine? Surgery?" Willie asked in desperation. His stalwart and the foundation for his future was crumbling before his eyes. She had supported him. She'd guided him through the darkness after his parents' death. She'd kept him out of trouble and helped him find the path he wished to seek.

"He says they are doing some advanced heart surgeries at the hospital but we won't be able pay for it. Don't even *think* of paying for it," Edna commanded and waved her index finger as if to scold Willie.

Willie tasted his own tears on his lips. "I know some people that can help you get the surgery. We won't have to pay a dime. I want to do this for you, Grandma. I'm a grown man," Willie cried.

"Willie, don't mortgage your future on the past. You've got promise. You've got my spirit and your mother and father's spirit. You'll be able to tackle any obstacle. Don't let my passing ruin you," she offered calmly and held her arms out for a hug.

Willie hung onto her tightly and whispered in her ear, "I'm not going to let you go. I want you to see my successes. Because my successes are due to your hard work. You mean so much to me."

The next morning while his grandmother was asleep, he called Dr. Stevenson. He asked him if Mr. Huberty could forego his school loan repayment and pay for his grandmother's surgery. A few days later when Willie came to the lab, Dr. Stevenson had a contract for him to sign that indicated that Alvin Huberty would pay for the surgery in exchange for services otherwise "not specified." After he signed the contract, Dr. Stevenson gave him a slightly thicker white envelope than previously. He told him to buy a box truck that would allow him to do food vending. Dr. Stevenson gave him the directions to the vending areas and the food distributors as well as a case holding vials of the food additive. The additive would be placed immediately after the food was prepared to prevent it from being broken down or denatured during the cooking process. He was also told to put it in a hidden place when not in use to prevent customers from seeing it. Willie took the case and ran the errands to begin his new job.

*   *   *

"Willie, now I know how and why you got involved," Jason began. "We need to expand more on this for the book. But I'm curious; why did you start selling newspapers?" He was intent on getting more of a personal angle to the story. Maybe it would reveal how this conspiracy had ruined America and as well as the promising life of a young man.

Willie finished his third Jack Daniel's and answered, "That's a story for another time. I want to get some rest and see Europe for the first time with some fresh eyes."

"But you can't leave me hanging—" Jason began.

Willie leaned his seat back and turned toward the aisle. He saw an unkempt obese man struggling to get into his seat. Willie closed his eyes and tried to forget the story he just told Jason.

Chapter 9

"I've never been able to get in your head."

"... The end." Charles finished reading from the large illustrated book and kissed his daughter on the forehead.

"But what about the princess? Did she have a pony? Were there dragons there?" Kelly asked. She had inherited the inquisitive nature of her father.

"*The end*, sweetie. They didn't say anything else. Maybe the dragons eat little girls past their bedtime," Charles smiled at Kelly.

"Daadddy! Use your 'magination!" Kelly screamed.

"That's for little girls to do when they go to sleep. You are incorrigible, you know that?" Charles got up to turn off the light.

"What's that mean?"

"Go to bed. Sleep tight." Charles shut the light off and as he exited her room, his cell phone went off. It was Daria's number. It had been nearly two months since they had spoken in the hotel room. He missed her but after the talk he had with Heather he became rededicated to their marriage. Charles felt like an addict wanting a cigarette or crack. He had kept Daria out of his head for what seemed like forever and now she was calling him. He let the cell phone ring until it went to voice mail.

Beep, beep, beep.

Their house was a two story, open layout, colonial home. Heather was in the kitchen washing dishes. She was scraping the dried cheese off the lasagna pan. Charles didn't know if Heather could hear the phone over the running water.

Beep, beep, beep.

"Honey, who's calling this late?" Heather yelled from the first floor.

"Just the speaker's bureau. I don't want to be bothered with them right now," Charles replied. He had cut back his speaking engagements to local venues in Philadelphia, Baltimore and Washington to ensure that he was safe at home by midnight, so this excuse was not unexpected. The encounter with Michael Goldberg had also rattled him and he liked to be accompanied by a male drug representative who sponsored the talks.

Beep. Beep. Beep.

Charles walked into the bathroom and turned on the sink. He opened the flip phone, and whispered, "Hello."

"Hi! I haven't heard from you in awhile. I miss you," Daria cooed. She sounded like the conversation in the hotel room in New Orleans had not happened.

"What? I can barely hear you. Where are you calling from?" Charles whispered firmly into the phone.

"I'm in a club. I want to see you again. Ha—" Daria yelled at the other end.

Charles sensed she was having a good time with her friends at a bar. He was irritated that she was yelling and giggling when he was trying to be covert.

"You said it was over and I accept that. So let's just leave it there," Charles insisted.

"What? I didn't hear you. Hey stop that," Daria laughed.

"I love my wife. Let's let it go at that. Goodbye." Charles folded the phone. When he opened the bathroom door, his wife was still cleaning in the kitchen.

"Are you almost done in there?" Charles shouted down to Heather.

"I'll be up in a couple of minutes," Heather yelled back.

Charles walked into the bedroom and changed into his pajamas.

*   *   *

He thought about Daria all night. What did she want? Why did she call when she was with friends at a bar? He hadn't thought about her in a long time and wondered why she'd forced herself into the picture again. Didn't she want out? Their relationship had come to a sudden end. Charles knew a breakup had been boiling away inside her for years. He knew it was inevitable because he had never planned on leaving his true love. *Maybe she was just drunk and felt like calling.*

When he woke up, he continued as if no one had called and got ready for the office. He knotted his blue tie around a white shirt collar. He put on his navy blazer, zipped up his blue pants, sprayed on some cologne and made his way to the kitchen to kiss his wife farewell.

"I'll see you at six, then," he said and smiled.

"Okay let me know when you're done. Make some people thin today," Heather replied with some pep. She had felt more invigorated now that she knew her husband was committed to her alone.

"I'll try." Charles closed the door behind him. He knew all day he would hate being awake, alone and not busy. Although driving took some contemplation, it didn't take away his thoughts about Daria's recent call. He didn't know why he continued to dwell on it. On occasion, since the breakup, he would think about a sinister connection between Daria, Michael Goldberg, and AGWorld and how it had been a good idea to quit the relationship anyway. He wondered if Daria was a siren dashing him against the hard rocks of corporate and government scandal. He didn't know anyone else at AGWorld. Perhaps the government thought he had stolen some corporate secrets. He remembered how that Hairston man had dragged Daria away from him the first time they met. *Why would the government be wary of a corporate secret? Oh of course, the government, AGWorld, Daria and Hairston are in cahoots. And I, Dr. Charles Mohr, am the keystone keeping their secrets about obesity and food additives quiet. Should I be so paranoid to wear a tin foil hat to keep them from reading my thoughts?* Charles giggled to himself as he closed the door of his silver Benz and walked into the weight loss center.

"Morning, Dr. Mohr," a nurse in purple scrubs chirped.

"Hi Jessica," Dr. Mohr replied.

"We have a couple of early birds here to see you. The patients are in rooms one and two," Jessica said.

Dr. Mohr started to see his patients. He would grab a manila chart and look at the notes and vitals already taken by the nurse and medical assistant. Many of his patients would show up early to find out the newest panacea to their weight problems. The options Dr. Mohr had at his disposal were gastric bypass surgery, medication, and good old fashioned diet and exercise. Except for the surgery, successful sustained weight loss was not common, especially for the largest of his patients, and he knew the futility of suggesting the non-surgical forms of therapy at the outset. He looked at the patient's chart in room one. She had half a dozen medications listed that were sequela of her weight.

"Hi, Dr. Charles Mohr, nice to meet you," Charles said and shook her hand. He sat on a small grey stool diagonally from his patient.

"Hi, Dr. Mohr, I'm Fanny Menendez," the patient answered as she shook his hand, remaining seated.

"Well, what brings you to our clinic today?" Dr. Mohr asked with a smile.

"Look at me. Can't you tell? I'm here to lose weight. Can you help me?" she asked with surprise. She couldn't understand why he was asking these questions when it was so obvious. This made her frown in frustration and her three chins quivered as she made each of the faces.

"Let me just find out a little about you and we can work out the options," Dr. Mohr stated calmly to ease her nerves. He then proceeded to ask her questions about her weight and the approximate amount of weight that she had gained over time.

She explained she had always been sort of heavy since the age of eighteen, around two hundred pounds, and that she gained the most weight with her three pregnancies, so that now she weighed closer to three hundred twenty pounds. Dr. Mohr discovered she had high blood pressure and diabetes and that her siblings and her parents were also heavy. After questioning her, he performed a physical examination. She struggled to get onto the exam table. He looked for any physical manifestations of an overt hormonal cause of her obesity but found none.

"Diets don't work for me. You know, I eat nothing but I still do not lose weight," she commented as she waddled back to the armless chair.

"Well, your body may have a slow metabolism, but really, you can't be making fat from nothing. If you were able to do that, you could solve the world's energy problems. It would be like cold fusion."

"Ohh. . .at least that would make me rich," she giggled. "I have tried this Slimcor stuff that they advertise on TV but that doesn't work for me. Are there any other medications that I can take before I get cut?" she asked, looking for a glimmer of hope before encountering a surgeon's knife.

"I don't think so. Of the medication options we have now, one can cause terrible diarrhea when you eat too much fat, and because you have high blood pressure you really can't take the other one," Dr. Mohr carefully explained. He then told her that surgery was the best option. He went through an anatomical chart of the different procedures. He told her the potential risks and the need for lifelong, daily ingestion of multiple small meals and vitamin supplements. While surgery was a large and risky procedure he had seen it work multiple times, but also had seen what had not gone so well. Usually, bad outcomes occurred because wounds in the skin or bowels did not heal appropriately. This didn't stop him from advising surgery to those whose heart could tolerate it, as it was the only way that he saw a majority of patients attain a substantial weight loss.

Mrs. Menendez listened carefully to Dr. Mohr's lecture and appeared agreeable to the surgery. "Well. I knew before coming here that this would be one of the options. And if you think I don't have too many other choices besides diet, I will go with the surgery," she agreed, expressionless, resigned to her fate. She had debated the options in her mind and the small risk of death on the operating table outweighed the possibility of a lifetime of painful arthritis and debilitating diabetes complications.

"All right, great. Mindy at the front desk will schedule you with the endocrinologist, cardiologist and surgeon. I will see you in the hospital and after the surgery they will make your follow-up appointment at the front desk. It was very nice to meet you." Charles shook Mrs. Menendez's hand as his cell phone began to ring. When she left the room he looked at it. It was Daria.

He opened the flip phone. "Hello," he whispered with some trepidation.

"Hi, it's me. I want to talk," Daria started with sadness in her voice.

"Daria, I can't right now. I'm in the middle of patients," Charles said with some forcefulness.

"Can we meet for lunch today?" she asked with hope.

"Where? I can't go too far. I have to see more people in the afternoon," Charles replied. He hoped it was close as he wanted to see her. He needed to know that his feelings for her were over and he thought he could do this by confronting his addiction head on. He also was curious. *She was the one that broke up with me, right?*

"How 'bout that diner outside Wilmington? I'm in D.C. now and I should make it there by noon," Daria asked with anticipation.

"Okay, sounds good, see you then. Bye," Charles closed the phone. "Great," he grumbled under his breath. "What did I just get myself into?" His heart started to race and he could feel the sweat on his forehead. He smiled to hide his anxiety as Jessica, his nurse assistant, passed.

Dr. Mohr continued to see his morning patients. He was constantly distracted by the thought of Daria. Obesity, his industry and place in life, was in front him and yet a million miles away. *Should I really be seeing her? I wish the patient sitting in front of me hadn't shown up for his appointment. I hope the next lady comes early.* He became very distant with his patients and didn't open himself up even to those he had seen for many years. The goal for him now was to see Daria at noon.

The ten minute drive to their meeting place seemed to take an hour. The four traffic lights on the way to the diner were major irritants. He nearly honked at an old woman in her Buick who didn't jump right off at the green light. The aqua and red diner came into view and Charles felt relief. He parked his car. A cool breeze helped in getting much needed air to his brain.

When he walked into the diner, Daria stood up from one of the booths. She wore a brown skirt suit with a light blue silk blouse. She looked just as beautiful as the night that she left him. Charles heard frying in the background and smelled the grease from the lunchtime meals. He walked up to her with his hands in his packets. "Hi," he said demurely.

"Charles, I'm so happy to see you. I'm sorry… about a few months ago," she offered with a smile and motioned for him to take a seat.

"Daria, you know you were right," Charles said, looking into her piercing gaze for a few seconds and then down at the menu, squinting at it as he was still standing.

"What do you mean? I was right? About what? I need to see you again," she said with a restrained voice. Her eyes hungered for a connection. She didn't flinch. She knew in the back of her mind, the sensible part of her brain that got her through her PhD, that this relationship was utterly ridiculous and untenable. She motioned to him to sit at the booth. Charles sat down with his hands still in his pockets.

"I mean, you were right in New Orleans. We shouldn't keep this up. It's not healthy. I love my wife. I love Heather. She knows about us or me with someone besides her--not necessarily you." Charles looked at her and then through her.

"Listen, you liked us as much as I did. You remember." She softly recounted their first night together while she rubbed his calf with her stocking-clad foot.

Charles did not respond to her advance. "I missed you at first. I see you for what you are now--an addiction. But I'm over it. You're young and accomplished. What are you doing with me, anyway? You were about to get married when I met you. If I was younger and not involved, I would," Charles explained and tried holding her hand.

"Thanks for the fucking lecture!" she yelled, eliciting stares from other customers. She was angered by his paternalistic excuses. She pulled her hand away from Charles. "Why did I even try? It was all their idea anyway. I was ready to let you go. Then they thought it would be beneficial for me and the company to be with you. 'Get in your head,' they said. I've never been able to get in your head. Ugh," she mumbled into her blouse. Her eyes darted back and forth with frustration.

"What? Huh? Who wanted us to be together? I thought it was about us," Charles asked, not because he had any future interest in her but he thought their affair had been genuine. He had a strong desire to know what it was she wanted from him. *Who would find our relationship beneficial?*

"No one. Nothing. I have to go." She picked up her bag, stood up, and stomped her heels into the linoleum floor as she walked out of the diner.

An older man with a grease-stained, white apron wrapped around his large belly came up to the table. "The missus not stayin' for lunch?" he asked while chewing on a toothpick. He held a pad and paper at the ready for Charles' order.

Charles held his hand up and grinned.

"Okay, buddy, take your time," the pudgy man sighed and walked back behind the counter, taking a slice of pie from under a glass case for himself.

Chapter 10

"I'm on to you."

Jason and Willie landed in the Zurich airport. Unlike Willie, Jason talked almost continuously about everything like a four-year-old child without an off switch. He darted from topic to topic covering everything from decorating his row home in South Philadelphia to his relationship with his girlfriend. Amongst the chit-chat, he tried to work his way into asking Willie about his grandmother and the food truck.

Willie looked around the airport and listened to all the interesting combinations of ethnicities and languages spoken by them. Africans were speaking French and Asians were speaking German. For a moment when he observed the disparate sights and sounds, it felt like watching a TV that was on the blink. He sank down in one of the many colorful airport chairs and realized how much of life he had missed in his depressive cocoon. He looked out through the expanse of glass in front of him at the tail fins of the aircraft with their white crosses on red backgrounds--the Swiss flag. He noticed how clean the airport was relative to Newark, New Jersey. The food court generated smells from all continents but smelled most overwhelmingly of butter and bread. Willie walked to a food court vendor, leaving Jason to find him. He bought a heavily buttered fresh baguette and started eating.

"Can I have some of that?" Jason panted. He had panicked at the thought of losing his traveling companion. He knew Stevenson wouldn't give him the story he needed without someone who had the goods on him, like Willie.

Willie continued to pan the airport looking at all the different people, indifferent to Jason, who was a fly in his ear.

"All right, I guess I'll get my own, but sharing would keep the weight off of us both," Jason smiled at the unresponsive Willie. "Well, let's go get our luggage," Jason suggested and tugged at Willie's brown leather jacket.

"Mmm," Willie grunted stuffing his mouth with food. He followed Jason to baggage claim. They waited quietly for their luggage and finished their bread. After picking up their luggage, they boarded a shiny red train headed for Lucerne.

*   *   *

"Aw, God! What an uncomfortable flight. They have to make those seats wider. Goldberg could have gotten us first class tickets. If we have to do this silly mission, we should be traveling in comfort," Tony complained, slowly trailing off into a grumble. He stretched his arms out, showing his yellow armpit sweat stains and twisted from right to left to loosen out his back. One of his shirt tails was sticking out of the front of his pants underneath his belly.

"You could always make yourself smaller," Elijah replied and cracked a rare smile. He threw out the *Washington Post* he had brought for his trip.

"Yeah, yeah, how am I gonna do that, magic? I gotta take a piss. Watch my case," Tony said and started to walk towards the men's room.

"Don't be too long. We need to take the train to Lucerne to keep an eye on these guys," Elijah replied, keeping an eye on Jason and Willie.

"Aw, shit! Not another freakin' long ride in tiny seats," Tony whined and looked back at Elijah, who was not paying attention to him.

"Hurry up," Elijah yelled.

*   *   *

Jason and Willie took their seats. They watched as a black man in a grey suit ran to catch the train with a heavy-set friend several steps behind him gasping for air. A conductor was just about to tell the engineer to get going when the two men finally made it on board.

"Those two men are still coming along with us, or at least trying," Jason remarked, remembering them from the flight.

"Who, what are you talking about?" Willie was still in a daze and couldn't remember the heavy man on the plane that had made him chuckle.

"The guys from our flight… Never mind them, you have to let me know how things worked out with the food truck before we meet Dr. Stevenson face-to-face," Jason insisted.

Willie looked out the window past Jason at the snow-capped Alps. "I guess you're right. It would make sense to go over the nitty-gritty before we see Stevenson."

✳   ✳   ✳

Willie picked up the case from Dr. Stevenson's desk. "So, Mr. Huberty will take care of everything?" he asked, hopefully.

"Don't worry about your grandmother, Willie. Just tell her to get to the University. The surgery will be taken care of. Just do *your* part, okay?" Dr. Stevenson put his hand on Willie's shoulder. He gave him a comforting wink.

Willie left the lab with the case of glass test tubes filled to the brim with yellow viscous fluid and passed the high school extern. The test tubes clinked away inside the wooden case. Willie felt self-conscious, knowing somehow what he was doing was not quite right. *My grandmother needs this surgery* rolled around in his brain.

"Hey Neptune, need help with that case?" a lanky white boy with excessive facial acne asked. The extern had been in awe of Willie since he started working at Dr. Stevenson's lab. He thought Willie was the epitome of cool in attitude and dress. For students at his all-white prep school, black was where it was at. Several of his friends had even tried growing Afros. He liked talking to Willie about the latest Jackson Five song or more risqué Al Green record. He also liked to hear about the rough life in the 'hood, though he didn't grasp that this distraction for him was a reality for many.

Willie came out of his trance. "Hey, hey, Charlie Brown. How's Snoopy doing?" Willie ignored Charles' offer with a locker room quip. He'd applied the cartoon reference to Charles because of the kid's slight tendency toward nerdiness and a-down-in-the dumps attitude. Willie knew that the kid idolized him but wished it was a cool kid that did so, not this introverted soul. Despite his nerdiness, he thought that maybe with a little work, he might make an all-right Robin to his Batman while he was there.

"If you mean the rat, the rat is doing fine," Charles answered flatly. He hated that Willie considered him a perennial loser and tried to separate himself from his comic-strip namesake. "Where are you going with that case?"

"Just some junk that Dr. Stevenson wanted me to get rid of," Willie said, wanting to change the subject.

"Oh--can I see? What is it?" Charles asked inquisitively. He wanted to be involved. Dr. Stevenson always seemed to have interesting projects for Willie to do. He, also, wanted some of Willie's cool to rub off on him and thought the more time he spent with him, eventually the cool would stick. He was a shy, smart kid who felt like he was the only high school sophomore that had never been on a date.

"It's not that kind of junk," Willie said sternly. "Hey, what have you got planned for the weekend?" Willie asked, to get him off of the subject.

Charles' face lit up. "My dad is coming home from another sales trip. So we're gonna' hang out some. Maybe go to an Orioles game," Charles said with glee.

"Sounds cool man. That AG-USA's keepin' him busy. They seem to be really movin' and shakin'," Willie remarked, not aware of Mr. Huberty's connection to the company that employed Charles' father.

"Yeah, he's on the road a lot. My folks usually fight when he gets back but me and my dad usually have a good time anyway. How 'bout yourself?" Charles asked.

"I got a date and some things I have to take care of for Dr. Stevenson. So let me get rid of this stuff. Let me know how things go with your dad," Willie said with a grin. Just as young Charles was envious of him, he yearned for the nuclear family that Charles had. If he couldn't get back the family destroyed by fire, maybe when things settled down he could start a family of his own. For now, he felt so much responsibility was thrust upon him.

"Okay, man," Charles replied awkwardly and watched as Willie walked down the hall with the case. He then returned to the feeding experiments with his rat. This particular day Charles was comparing chemicals that enhanced feeding in rats. Unfortunately for the rats, after they were observed alive, the rats' brains were dissected in order to find neurochemical reasons for the enhanced feeding.

Willie walked down to his Lincoln and loaded the case in the trunk. His next trip was to the commercial vehicle store. He bought the model Mr. Huberty had recommended. He left the case in the truck in the sales lot and drove home in his Lincoln. The next morning he would catch a bus to the sales lot and get the truck loaded with food.

*   *   *

"You know, it's amazing how all these accomplished people start out kind of dorky," Jason quipped.

Willie's concentration was not broken. He took a travel guide from the pocket in front of him. He saw a list of different skiing venues. All the people in the pictures were blonde and beautiful and were having the time of their lives. *Why some live in leisure and others toil is just inexplicable and just a matter of who gets the best fairy dust.* Willie continued his story.

*   *   *

Willie pulled his truck into the Vincent Mauriello food distribution center where they loaded his truck with all the goods he would need to supply his customers with lunch. They loaded sandwich meats, burgers, hot dogs, frozen fries, breads, and desert cakes. He had done some short-order cooking when he was in high school and so he was not unfamiliar with what he needed or how to get the job done.

"Hey, don't I know you?" asked a man in blue overalls.

"Hey Jerome, has this been what you've doing with yourself after high school?" Willie asked and smiled, happy to see a familiar, beaming face. Jerome was a distant cousin he'd gone to high school with. Willie shook his hand firmly with both hands. Jerome didn't settle for a handshake and brought him in for a quick hug and pat on the back.

"Yeah, I heard a few months ago that you were going to business school. What are doing with a food truck?" Jerome asked. He started loading the food truck with rolls and boxes of condiments.

"Well, it helps pay the school bills. I'm not giving up on that business school. What about you? What are you doing here?" Willie asked to change the subject. Realistically he was unsure of his future in business school. He'd brushed his dreams aside and focused on his grandmother's health for the time being. He wasn't one to ask for help or ask for charity so he kept his grandmother's cardiac condition and his finances to himself.

"Man, I'm not college material. There ain't no jobs out there. I hear that you're going to the docks. I don't know what you're gonna make sellin' out there. I know a few brothers there that lost their jobs recently. Pretty soon there will be no economy for your business degree," Jerome negatively noted.

Willie didn't know whether the last statement was fact or Jerome bringing down his future job prospects due to envy. The mid-seventies were not economically kind to any American but they were worst for urban Americans of color. "I think I'll be able to make a buck or two. Hey Jerome, if you had a chance to help a sick relative but say had to do something that may be questionable, would you do it? Or more specifically, how about say you put something in someone's food without them knowing it, but it was not harmful to them?" Willie asked trying to get the support of the common man.

Jerome furrowed his brow in thought and then raised his right eyebrow while looking at Willie. "I don't know man. Sounds a little like that Tuskeegee shit; one of the few good things Nixon did for our people." The Tuskeegee syphilis study Jerome hinted at had documented the natural course of the disease in African-Americans. Despite the availability of a viable treatment for syphilis, they were not given the treatment, unbeknownst to them. Researchers then studied the late stages of the disease. It was a landmark mistake that helped in the creation of review boards for all studies and the process whereby research subjects were informed that they were in a study.

"I don't know, man," Jerome continued. "I guess it depends on the relative, I guess. Are you addin' something to this food? Better be spices 'cause this food is bland. Believe me. I work here. Heh. Heh. You're *better off* adding something," Jerome laughed. He finished loading the rest of the food into the box truck.

"Yeah, I better find that super spice or I'm gonna go broke," Willie said with a forced smile. Willie turned from Jerome and closed the truck doors.

"Good luck, man," Jerome laughed and patted Willie on the back.

Willie grinned and waved goodbye. He jumped in the box truck and turned the engine over. He headed out of the parking lot and made it onto I-95 to the Port of Baltimore.

Willie pulled into the outermost portion of the parking lot for the loading facilities. It was only ten o'clock so he was able to take his time getting ready for lunch. He watched the cranes lifting large multicolored steel boxes on or off of large ships with what seemed like military precision. Men in jeans and vests with reflective stripes for safety walked around the loading area. From a distance, it looked like a light show with the men in bright yellow helmets bobbing among the dark containers. The yard was a mini roadway with trucks depositing or receiving cargo boxes. Away from the shipyard were old, large, brick storage facilities that were still somewhat actively used. Willie thought of all the history of these warehouses and how the large buildings were filled with the sweat of the old stevedoring days before the cranes. He cracked open a window to let in some air but the air that seeped in was filled with diesel fumes. The subdued rumble when the box truck's cabin was closed turned into a cacophony of clanking steel after Willie opened a window.

Willie walked to the back of the truck and took out the food and the additive. Dr. Stevenson had told him to add it to the carbohydrates, starches and sugars in the lunch bread and the soda. He poured one test tube into a plastic ketchup bottle. He started the deep fryer containing a couple of sticks of lard and cleaned the hot plate with his spatula. The air became thick with the smell of the fryer. He was nearly complete in his preparation and put his attention toward opening the long service gate next to the grill. The crank was hard for Willie to turn despite being generously greased. He eventually got it open, flooding the immediate area with the smell of fried food.

Willie looked out the serving window that faced the activities of the long-shoremen. The containers came up and down from the cranes. The names read Hyundai, Mitsubishi, Sealand, Maersk, and Yang Ming. He wondered what the containers had in them and where they had been. He hoped that he could one day go to some of the exotic places that these goods had come from. He began to see many of the men looking at their watches and then glancing in his direction. Willie's box truck was in the appropriate area for the food trucks. There was a Chinese food truck one hundred feet away to his left and a Greek sandwich truck about fifty feet to his right.

A shrill loud whistle blew and the men came toward the trucks. Some of them had metal lunch pails and sat on benches by the trucks. About half of the men headed for the three trucks. The men divided into three groups.

"Hey Al, a new food truck," someone in the bunch yelled.

"Yeah, let's check it out," another voice answered.

"How are you guys doing? Welcome to Neptune's food truck, all ready for lunch," Willie said.

A grumble came from the men. They started to line up at the counter. "Hey fellas, wait a minute, ladies first," a man bellowed toward the back.

"Go on Liz," another man said.

A thin woman approached the van. She had feathered hair that peeked through the bottom of her yellow helmet. She had a faint mole at the right corner of her lips which had wrinkles surrounding it from years of smoking. She looked a hard worker in her mid-forties.

"Hi! What can I get for you ma'am?" Willie asked. He looked at her tan work boots that didn't seem to go with her skinny, jean-clad legs.

"Hey, handsome, can I get a hot dog with relish and mustard and a soda, please?" she ordered in a harsh, long-term smoker's voice. She smiled, faintly embarrassed at being hauled up to the front of the line by the men.

Willie took one of the hot dogs off of the grill. He put it on a bun and then placed his hand on the ketchup container with the sauce. He had his back turned to prevent people from viewing his experimental addition. He then turned with his hand on the bottle at the woman with her hand on the counter looking out at the container ship. It looked to Willie like she was trying to get some distance from her colleagues. *She was as much a loner in this world as I feel in mine.* He took his hand off the additive and squirted on the mustard and relish. He gave her the hot dog and soda and she gave him the seventy-five cents for the food.

"How is it?" the large white man waiting behind her asked.

"Not bad," Liz answered with her mouth half full.

"Gimme a burger and make it quick, buddy," the man grunted with an angry grin on his face.

Unlike Liz, Willie found no personal connection with this man and quickly made his burger. He put the additive on the bun and added it to the soda he ordered as well. They all came and ordered: Dave, Ed, George, Fred, Lamont, Roger, Hector, Dwayne, Burt, Al. He kept track of them all and who did and who he didn't give the additive to. He began to notice that men who didn't get the additive weren't coming as often as those who did. The additive drew men away from their usual lunch routine at either the Greek or Chinese place or even the packed lunch made by their wives. Many other trucks serving similar American fare left the lot due to a lack of customers. Soon, the Greek truck had moved five hundred feet away to try to attract more business. The Chinese truck held firm.

After a month went by many of the men who received the additive looked as if they had tighter jeans. His business was very steady. The Greek truck left for another, more lucrative pier. Willie was feeling pretty good, and each week he gave his observational analysis to Dr. Stevenson who showered him with praise. *My Grandma is going to be OK,* he would think after doing this.

Within a few months of attracting seventy percent of the business on the dock, Willie heard a knock on the back door of the food truck. "Hello?" Willie called as he opened the door. He wondered if he should open the door as it could be an inspector or worse a robber taking his truck, cash and the additive. Instead, it was a thin Chinese man in his sixties with a large wooden spoon in his hand.

"No hello. You take away my business!" he spat in a shrill, broken English voice and hit Willie in the forehead with the spoon. He then entered the back of the van.

"Ow! Whoa man. Calm down," Willie said and rubbed the spot on his forehead where the spoon hit. He smelled Chinese food coming from the man's clothes. Willie could have broken the little man in half but he didn't want any trouble. He knew also that he had an unfair advantage in the food truck war.

"No calm down. You take away *my* business. What you using in your food? MSG? I use MSG but losing business to you. Jerk," he scowled and looked around the van.

He then grabbed the yellow liquid that Willie had transferred to a ketchup container. Willie's heart was about to come out of his chest. He was going to be discovered. The old man took a whiff of the container. He threw it down on the ground.

"Nothing. Arrgh! You take away my business. I need to feed my family too," he growled.

"Listen man. They just like my food better. That's all," Willie reassured him calmly.

"I'm on to you," the old man squinted at him and walked out the door slamming it behind him.

Willie sat in the driver's seat and let out a sigh. He watched the owner of the Chinese truck get back in his vehicle. The truck kept coming to his pier for a few more weeks but soon retreated as the Greek truck had done. The business was really picking up now. The imposing men that he was serving were getting much larger in the middle. He would again give his data to Dr. Stevenson. Every week he would do this until one day six months into his truck business he found a note on the lab door. It was an envelope with "To Willie" written on it. He opened it.

Dear Willie,

You did a wonderful job. The stuff really works. I am going to start working for AG-USA but please send all your future notes to the address below. You will get any further instructions by mail. Keep up the good work. Sorry for the hasty retreat.
Your friend,
John

Willie continued to travel to the shipyard for the next few weeks. John's departure from the lab was a surprise to him. Willie had thought that this commercial food additive study would be a way for Stevenson to subsidize basic science lab experiments and that the Doctor would be spending more time in the lab, not leave. In the last few weeks prior to the letter, Stevenson had become less communicative. He made no mention of the food additive or of a desire to leave his research. Willie's interactions with him had become more distant than when he first opened the food truck. He would give Stevenson the data or leave it on his desk without feedback from him. The two had still been going out for an occasional drink, with another lab worker present, and often discussed current events, like the Redskins, Colts, or Orioles games. Willie wondered about Dr. Stevenson's sudden career change: *Maybe he got more money with Ag-USA? Maybe he had a better lab at Ag-USA? Why did he stop talking to me about the additive? As a mentor and friend, why didn't he leave me any contact information?*

Willie sent the study results to the post office box listed for Mr. Huberty in the note. Everything was to Mr. Huberty's specifications so that he would follow through on covering his grandmother's surgery. Her surgery date was coming soon. Over the last six months she was being admitted frequently for intravenous fluid removal. When she was at home, she slept. At times, Willie thought she might not survive to her surgery. One of the days he was at home tending to her, a letter without return address came to him.

It read:

Willie,
Your help has been greatly appreciated. Sell or keep the rest of the food. Leave the additive in the truck and have the entire truck disposed of at the below junk yard. Tell them I told you to have it crushed. Your grandmother's surgery is taken care of as well as a few weeks of after care. Best of luck in your future endeavors.
AH

Willie sold the last of the food in the truck. He then drove it to the junk yard listed in the note. He parked the van and approached a man in grey overalls rummaging through a pile of old auto parts. In the background, Willie could hear the squeal of crushed metal and glass in a car compactor.

"Hi! A Mr. Huberty sent me to dispose of this box truck," Willie said.

"Right, crushed. Leave the keys in the car," he continued to paw through the parts as if Willie was not there.

"Thing is, he changed his mind," Willie asserted, with slight trepidation in his voice.

The man with a grey crew cut stood up. He had a name tag that read "Bud." He looked straight into Willie's eyes to discern the truth. "He changed his mind?" Bud asked and gave him a long, hard stare

"Yeah, Mr. Huberty was in a generous mood. He said you can hold onto it and use it for parts. He has several other trucks that might need them as well and he has nowhere to store this thing," Willie lied without flinching.

"Fine whatever, just leave the keys in the truck," Bud said and went back to his pile.

Willie headed for the bus stop and passed by the carcass of a Lincoln Continental that had just been totaled. He thought the truck could come in handy to him in the future.

*   *   *

"So why didn't you do what Huberty asked?" Jason asked.

"I needed some collateral for my grandmother's surgery," Willie replied as he looked out the window.

"And so what happened to your grandmother?" Jason asked. He tried again to break this hard-to-crack nut.

"I'll let you know when I feel like it. You've got your story. We'll talk to Dr. Stevenson and we'll be done with it. Just leave my grandmother out of your *New York Times* Bestseller List," Willie spat.

"I'm… Willie… I'm sorry. I am curious to know, just to build a better picture of you. A man is a sum of his parts and she, and this experience have shaped you. That's all I'm trying to get at," Jason explained as he put his hand on Willie's forearm.

At that moment the train stopped and the doors opened efficiently. Willie and Jason stepped out onto the Lucerne platform. The air was cool but not chilly and the sun peeked through the clouds. Just before the doors closed the agents got off the train, keeping Willie and Jason in sight from a distance.

Chapter 11

"Well then I will let him know that things will be taken care of."

Mike Goldberg sat in his downsized office in the J. Edgar Hoover building in Washington. He looked over the case file of some jewelry thieves that were plaguing the Northeast. One side of his desk was dedicated to this case, the other was a credit card scam. The reams of paper were piled a foot high in some places--evidence and bureaucratic forms made up most of it. Detective Goldberg knew when things really needed to be taken care of, as those matters didn't go through the usual channels of days if not weeks of paperwork and authorizations. If this were Clinton's jewelry or Bush's credit cards, the gloves would be off.

His office had gotten smaller with the creation of the Department of Homeland Security. It had an eight-by-eight picture of the godfather of the FBI, J. Edgar Hoover, on one wall and on the other "the untouchable" Eliot Ness. The rest of his office was relatively bare. He was divorced and did not have any children. He was unfortunately a man whose relatively secretive job was also his hobby.

The main lights were off in the office and the room was windowless. It had been a week since the work order was placed for the flickering fluorescent lights. Michael had no patience for this and just shut it off. Although his building had been smoke-free for many years, the smell of cigarette smoke filled the air when he was stressed. The only light in the office was supplied from two accountants' lamps. The green-back light and the smoke gave the aura of an old fashioned basement poker game.

The second lamp came from a carrel on the northeast corner of his office. It was the "office" of Dirk Meal. He had suffered the most after the reorganization. He hated the smell of the smoke but didn't want to peeve his boss. He believed the fastest way to get out of the situation was to deal with his current station. On his desk was a photo of himself, his wife, and their three children. His carrel was significantly smaller than Michael's imposing desk and he adapted to it by keeping it very neat and clean. He was typing up a recent briefing of the jewelry case for a meeting the next day. He was a big man. He was also a bit claustrophobic, and by burying himself in the computer, he could avoid having to acknowledge his close quarters.

There was a rap on the door. Dirk got up from his carrel, nearly hitting his head on the shelf above him. He opened the door which flooded the dark room with light. Dirk squinted at the thin silhouette that stood in the doorway.

"Marc, how are things? Come in. I'd offer you a seat but as you can see there isn't much room for one," Mike called from his desk.

Marc walked in and Dirk went back to work on other cases.

"Hi, Mike, how are things going on the case?" Marc Olesson asked. Marc knew only of the vague investigation that Mr. Irving wanted him to perform. From other staffers of other politicians he knew that Mike and Dirk were a political clean-up crew. They took side money to investigate political enemies or silence personal "problems," such as secret girlfriends. He stood in front of Mike's desk and observed the room's darkness and correlated it with a lack of funding tied to a lack of government, on-the-books work.

"My boys are in Lucerne, Switzerland following our friends," Mike said with confidence.

"My boss has a message for you." Marc handed Mike an envelope.

Mike leaned back in his chair putting his full weight behind him, nearly toppling the chair. The heavy base, however, did not move. His feet came up and rested on the top of his desk. A few files fell on the floor. "Don't worry about those," Mike waved and picked up a silver letter opener from his desk. Mike read the note quietly.

Michael,
Do not like the way things are progressing. Please consider a permanent solution to my predicament. Look forward to your efficient handling of the situation.
GI

"Have you gone over the contents of this letter with your boss?" Mike asked, knowing that "efficient" meant that people with information on Gordon Irving needed to be permanently silenced.

"Not exactly," Marc replied.

"Good, well, let him know we aim to please and we'll do our best to accommodate him. And by the way, let him know that I had a discussion with Dr. Mohr and he is out of the loop. He is not worth bothering with," Mike said with a smile.

"Well, then, I will let him know the updates and that things will be taken care of," Marc assured and nodded his head.

"Good luck at the party convention," Michael said.

"Thanks," replied Marc. Marc did not like the covertness of any of this. He didn't mind the occasional white lies or the "out-of-context" comments but didn't like how this was going. This was going to be someone's hide--literally. He wanted to know very little and get out of this room as quickly as possible. Marc walked out of the office.

"Good news, boss?" Dirk asked as he closed the door.

"Give a call to the boys. We need to talk after they get information from Stevenson," Michael said. Michael wiggled his feet and more files fell from his desk.

"Will do," Dirk replied. Dirk saved the work on his cases and left the office to perform his task.

Chapter 12

"Wouldn't it be nice if your Brussels sprouts tasted better? I didn't come up with the plan. I finished a crude idea and then Willie ran with it."

It was cool day in Lucerne. A slight breeze was blowing. Jason and Willie took a cab to their hotel. They felt the transition from paved to cobbled stone streets. There was a beautiful view of the lake and river that connected to it. The cab stopped at a small medieval style home of tan stucco and white wood molding. The molding had intricate shapes at the edges. The two got out of the cab and gave the cabbie his fare in Euros. They walked up a couple of steps to the hotel entrance. A bell man in a gold buttoned uniform and hat opened the door for them.

"Guten tag!" the doorman said with a smile.

"Thanks," Jason replied.

Willie nodded to the man and carried his suitcase to the check-in desk.

They went to their room which had two double beds. The room smelled of bathroom cleaner and potpourri. There were two windows that had been left open. They had a beautiful view of the lake and the mountains that drained into it.

"This view is gorgeous," Willie marveled with his mouth open.

"No time for that, the company only paid for two nights. I am not going to pay for another, especially with the exchange rate these days. Willie, could you hand me the map that's in your suitcase?" Jason asked. He liked going to exotic locales but right now he wanted to get this story done. His mind was also hounded by impending wedding plans put forth by his fiancé, a wedding he and she wanted to keep small but their respective families wanted to make enormous.

"Here you go," Willie said and went back to looking out the window.

"Well it shouldn't be too hard to find. Oh there it is. It's only a couple of blocks away from here," Jason proclaimed enthusiastically.

"You found him," Willie said.

"Yeah, let's go," Jason jumped up and headed for the door.

Willie followed slowly.

"Come on," Jason coaxed, as if they were going to miss a once-in-a-lifetime event.

"Do we even know he's home?" Willie questioned.

"Well we won't know until we get there. Personally, I don't want to warn him of our impending inquisition," Jason said, practically.

"That's probably a good idea," Willie agreed and picked up the pace with Jason.

They walked down the stairs to the main lobby. The doorman opened the door and they headed toward Dr. Stevenson's last known residence. Willie looked at all of the colors. The houses were so intricate. Willie imagined unrealistic perfect looking dolls coming from these doll houses. This was not like Willie's neighborhood in Washington where homes were non-picturesque dwellings that barely functioned in that capacity. Most of the homes here looked like they came from the medieval era, although there was an occasional modern home with various angles and sharp corners. They soon made it to an area made up mainly of shops. The stores all had large plate glass windows displaying all types of watches and jewelry. Tourists walked the streets with their cameras attached to their necks, peering into the windows. They turned down a quiet alley without shops. The alley had a number of metal fire escapes. The walls were brick and one wall was painted black.

Metal garbage containers in the alley made the alley reek. This was the first bad smell they had encountered since landing in Switzerland. The weather on the main street appeared to be partly cloudy with the sun breaking out but in the alley, it seemed very grey.

"This looks like it," Jason said.

Willie put his arm up blocking Jason's passage forward. "How did you find his whereabouts when no one else did?"

Jason began, "Someone close to Mr. Irving. Let's say in a chief of staff position told me to eat at a little mom-and-pop Indian restaurant in the area and ask about Stevenson."

"His chief of staff told you to eat at an Indian restaurant in Switzerland?" Willie looked down shook his head and smiled.

"I tried getting the food additive story from Gordon Irving himself. After a couple of times being denied for interview, his chief of staff sent me a note that the information I want could be gathered through Stevenson. He couldn't give me a direct address. Apparently, Stevenson frequents this Indian place. The workers seem to know him well and gave me this address."

Willie put down his arm and they walked a few more steps until they faced a black door with oxidized brass numbers reading one hundred and twenty-eight.

"Go ahead Willie, knock," Jason said. He made a face as if to tell him to hurry up.

Willie knocked on the door.

"Go away. This isn't a jewelry store," came a voice from inside.

"Dr. Stevenson. It's Willie Barnes. I thought we could go out for a drink," Willie yelled.

The brass knob of the metal door turned.

*　　*　　*

"What's news?" Tony asked.

"Looks like Goldberg wants us find out what they are saying to Stevenson," Elijah answered. They sat in their rental Peugeot 206 that was parked near the alley. Elijah peeked through his binoculars. He could see that the door had opened and Willie was talking to someone. Jason had leaned up against the wall next to the door so that whomever Willie was speaking to couldn't see Elijah.

Tony struggled once again with the cramped conditions. "God, the French must be tiny. Give me a Hummer or an Excursion any day," Tony noted. "So do we head back?" Tony asked hopefully and tried to untangle himself from the seatbelt.

"No, *we* talk to Stevenson after those two leave and then we get back," Elijah said firmly and pushed the seat belt release for Tony.

"Thanks," Tony answered and exhaled deeply.

$$*\quad*\quad*$$

"Willie, it's you! How are you old boy?" the old man exclaimed as if Willie were a chum from his *alma mater* Harvard. The man had long grey hair with a mangy looking beard, as if he was a West Virginia moonshiner. His hair was balding around his part. He was gaunt and wore a dirty grey shirt with faded blue pants. His bony feet were bare.

"Dr. Stevenson? It's nice to see you, sir," Willie replied. He looked at Dr. Stevenson blankly. He remembered the other relationships that tied in with Dr. Stevenson, like his grandmother, and the reason he and Jason had come to find him; the possibility that he had helped fuel the obesity epidemic.

"My dear Willie Barnes, are you here to do some wheeling and dealing with Credit Suisse? I had high hopes for you. So what brings you—" Dr. Stevenson stopped in mid-sentence as he looked toward the right door jamb. "Willie, who is this?" Dr. Stevenson asked. His forehead furrowed as he looked at Jason hiding behind the wall.

"He's a reporter," Willie said.

Dr. Stevenson quickly tried to close the door but Willie's foot blocked him.

"His name is Jason Lieberman. He wants to know about the additive," Willie insisted coldly.

"Willie, why did you bring him here? This is an exposé artist. I know his work. I don't want to be implicated in anything," Dr. Stevenson replied, trembling.

Jason put himself between Willie and Dr. Stevenson and put his hand on the door. "Dr. Stevenson, you were implicated when you asked Willie to put those chemicals in that food," Jason said forcefully.

Dr. Stevenson looked over Jason's arm and straight into Willie's eyes. He knew the world had cracked his shell. The past had become present. The best-case scenario for him would be to give up his information and go back to being a near-hermit. He was old, and maybe near death. Maybe letting the truth out now would give him eternal rest.

"Come in," Dr. Stevenson offered with a defeated quality and motioned with his arm to them.

The door opened into a very dark house. The house was of cinder block construction and the blocks were painted grey. The room was lit by a couple of fifty-watt incandescent bulbs on plain lamps with no covers. The windows were large warehouse types. Some of them were frosted and others were so dirty one could barely see through them. Even if someone did look through, the windows faced the surrounding brick buildings. There were no pictures hanging on the walls. There was one plant in a corner that looked as if it wasn't getting enough light or water. In the far corner from the entrance came a small amount of natural light. The floors were white linoleum that looked as though they had recently been mopped.

"So how did you get here?" Willie asked uncomfortably, as this was no longer a social call, especially with Jason there.

"I just left, you know—" Dr. Stevenson replied before he was cut off.

"Let's just get to the facts. We don't have much time, Willie. Let's at least get the information we want and then we'll expand on the story of Dr. Stevenson's life. We need to know about the additive," Jason said to the both of them.

Willie looked at him puzzled. Jason had kept pressing him about his grandmother's death. Willie thought this fact was extraneous to the story of the additive. *Why the hell doesn't he want to hear of Dr. Stevenson's fall? Jason wanted to know my back story--why not hear about Stevenson's? I want to hear about it. Why would he be living like this? He was a great scientist. He had a family. He was my friend.* He began to feel that Jason only wanted to know his personal story so that he could incriminate his friends. Willie went along with Jason's inquisition to see where it would lead.

"What Jason wants to know about is the liquid that we gave to the dock workers," Willie explained more calmly to Dr. Stevenson.

"Yes, well, I had been studying feeding habits in mice and rats, when I received a message from someone at AG-USA that you may now know as AGWorld. I was just near the end of my grant funding and my future grants had been rejected. I was in a bit of a rut. The person at AG-USA was going to sponsor all of my rodent work as long as I worked on a few samples of theirs. Most of their work I did myself but some of the more menial tasks I farmed out to some high school student."

"Charlie Mohr," Willie said with a smile and shook his head.

"I believe he preferred Charles. But anyway, I found the samples that they had given me promoted feeding. The effect was not only instantaneous but appeared as if it persisted after the additive was removed. What I mean by this is that rodents exposed to multiple doses continued to eat when doses were stopped. It was as if their appetite centers were permanently turned on."

"Who at AG-USA had given you the samples? Was it Mr. Huberty?" Jason inquired.

"Yes it was him. He was the science officer on the project. I heard he recently passed away," Dr. Stevenson said.

"He was in a nasty car accident about three years ago. It was a hit and run, actually," Jason replied.

Dr. Stevenson looked at Jason, surprised that it was that long ago, and nodded. "Hmm. I guess things happen. Anyway, he told me that he wanted to start seeing the effects in humans. I was not a human subject researcher. He said it wouldn't be a real experiment, more of a survey. He would come up with a skeleton of the plan. He wanted me to come up with some of the observational techniques and to document the folks who ate the additive. I felt ethically uncomfortable with actually doing the 'survey.' So I gave the task to Willie," Dr. Stevenson explained coldly.

If Willie were white, he would have looked beet-red. He was angered by this. Dr. Stevenson had not just given him some extra money, he'd been clearing his conscience. "Thanks for letting me do your dirty work," Willie sighed and leaned back in his chair with his knees apart.

"Willie, you knew human nature and were a keen observer in my lab. I also remembered that you were a short order cook in high school. You were close by and because of the impulsiveness of your age, I figure it would be easy to entice you into the project, especially with the advance," Dr. Stevenson explained very frankly.

"Some friend. Did you know that it was a real experiment? What about the promise and the ideas that I had for the future? Was that just to butter me up so that I could be *your* Tuskegee Institute? The dock workers were nice people, good people. They worked hard day in and day out," Willie interrupted Dr. Stevenson in the midst of his methodical excuses..

"Willie, you took part in the crime. You can sue the gun manufacturer but the killer pulled the trigger. It wasn't like you did it once or twice. You were there for six whole months. We made the calls to that stupid bar where you used to hang out to give you different variations of the formula. Don't lay this all on me. We did what we could to get what we wanted with a *harmless* food additive," Dr. Stevenson explained.

"Dr. Stevenson, you make it sound so harmless. You tell the millions of people that are obese whether they would trade the infirmities of diabetes, heart disease and cancer, associated with obesity, for good health," Jason interjected.

"Ha, ha--are you kidding me? You want to blame me for all of those diseases? Are you mad? These diseases are multifactorial. I am a mere mortal. You are accusing me of Hitler-esque genocide. My intentions were *not* to produce a killing machine. Besides it was AG-USA or AGWorld, whatever it is now, that came up with the plan. Talk to them. They told us everything was on the up-and-up. All the papers were filed with the FDA. So then it is the government's fault," Dr. Stevenson said gasping for breath. While he spoke he began to motion with his hands to himself and to the world. He then dabbed his forehead with a napkin that was on his coffee table to wipe away the perspiration collecting there.

"If you weren't Hitler, maybe you were Goebbels. You had a part. When I get this book out everyone will know. Hopefully some obese people will feel better knowing they are not all to blame. Maybe some of them will even hang your picture on their dartboard to exert some of their frustrations. You were integral, Dr. Stevenson," Jason said hyperbolically.

"This is too much. I am not to blame. You make it sound like I wanted to exterminate people. Wouldn't it be nice if your Brussels sprouts tasted better? I didn't come up with the plan. I finished a crude idea and then Willie ran with it. I was about to stop researching altogether. Money was flowing by the truck-load into heart disease and cancer. The study of weight was of little importance. They got my lab back on track. But I lost focus after the additive took off. I ignored my family. I went on all-night parties with AG-USA execs. It's all done. What's past is past. But I am not to blame. I was not integral. Maybe it's time you should go," Dr. Stevenson vacillated between ideas and began to get up from the couch.

Jason looked him in the eye. "Some person's good is another person's evil. Who was integral, if it wasn't you?" he asked, trying to wring the answer he wanted from Dr. Stevenson.

Dr. Stevenson was hunched over. He seemed to have aged during the conversation. The two men starred at him with laser-like focus.

"Mr. Irving was the one. It was not me. He is a very talented character that has good business knowledge and, for someone not formally trained, good science knowledge as well. He is your man," Dr. Stevenson said.

"Gordon Irving came up with everything?" Jason asked, surprised but pleased at the high profile of the name.

"Yes," Dr Stevenson said with a sigh as if an enormous weight had been lifted off of him. "Mr. Irving was very involved, via his mouthpiece, Mr. Huberty."

"So what was his stake in the additive?" Jason asked as he mentally zeroed in on the kill.

"Mr. Irving was at the time CEO of AG-USA. His father was on the board and he had a meteoric rise to the chairmanship at a very young age. There was a glut in corn production and not enough people to eat it. So he thought of a way to get them to eat it," Dr. Stevenson explained.

"Huh, just couldn't give it away. I'm sure a few million starving African kids could have used it," Willie scoffed.

HOW WE BECAME FAT

"That's not in the nature of corporate execs. At least not back then Willie. I would say he is a great soothsayer. In the research labs of AG-USA headquarters, they had been working on food additives that were a derivative of corn syrup. Using some of my early work on rat feeding behavior, he saw the voracious nature that these additives could produce. He also saw that the food additive caused an addiction to food long after it was removed," Dr. Stevenson said.

"So this effect was prolonged. And the rats got fatter?" Jason asked.

"Several times larger than those that did not have the additive," Dr. Stevenson responded. "His understanding of the medical world was very wide-reaching and it needed to be, as he served on a pharmaceutical company board while he was chair of AG-USA."

"He made a connection between obesity and disease?" Jason asked puzzled.

"More like he made a connection between the almighty dollar and human suffering," Willie sneered.

"He knew he could benefit from a market that he created, yes," Dr. Stevenson said and lowered his head.

The three men spent a while discussing the intertwining nature of obesity and illness. Dr. Stevenson told them about potential agents that Irving and his pharmaceutical friends were working on for weight loss and diabetes that would have come out five to seven years down the road after introduction of the additive in the food supply. Irving had anticipated the increase in these disorders from the food additive and also anticipated the wait time for FDA approval. These agents would be released to coincide with the onslaught of obesity-related disorders. The patents on the drugs would have lasted another decade, raking in profits for the companies for many years.

"Oh my goodness, Johnnie, you did not tell me we had guests," cooed a thin Indian woman with long black hair in her mid-forties as she entered the dark room. She tried straightening herself up in the presence of the surprise visitors and held her hands close to the v-opening of her blouse.

Willie and Jason stood up as they were also surprised.

"Jason and Willie, meet my girlfriend Sonal Patel. She looks after me or else I would be living in even more of a sty than you see here," Dr. Stevenson said.

"I am glad to see you all here. I have never seen Johnnie talk with anyone but me since I have known him. He has always been so reclusive. Where are you from? Would you like me to put on some tea?" she asked politely with a smile.

"Washington," Willie answered nervously as if he felt a little out of place.

"Philadelphia. We would love some tea. Thank you," Jason replied and smiled at her.

"I'll be back with the tea. Please sit down," she said. She walked back into the kitchen and from there she yelled, "Johnnie, did you get the tea from the grocery store?"

"No dear," Dr. Stevenson yelled back.

A few moments later she came out in a brown sweater jacket. "I'm going to the store. We have nothing in the house for your friends to eat," she explained with a frown on her face.

"Oh, please don't go, we don't need anything," Jason insisted.

"Nonsense, you are guests. It won't be a minute," Sonal insisted, displaying her Indian hospitality. She opened the door and headed to the store.

Willie looked at Dr. Stevenson, "Why did you turn away from your old life? You had a good family, a perfect family. You had joined up with AG-USA after the experiment. Then you just disappeared. Now you have a girlfriend in a little hole in the wall in Switzerland of all places."

Dr. Stevenson looked down at his chest and did not answer right away.

Jason looked at Dr. Stevenson as well. "I think I know why Willie. You see Dr. Stevenson had a vision just like Mr. Irving. The problem is that Dr. Stevenson's conscience finally caught up with him. He knew how the dominoes were falling and what he and Mr. Irving had caused. Isn't that right Dr. Stevenson?"

Dr. Stevenson stood up and put his hands in his pockets. He walked to one of the windows of his apartment that faced a brick wall and looked out. "I needed to clear my head. I had seen the ripple effect that the additive had caused. The company's profits were soaring. I had then found out how Irving was double dipping with his interests in the pharmaceutical industry. People were slowly killing themselves with food. I came here without telling anyone. One year became a dozen very quickly. I met Sonal at her parents' restaurant that I frequented. She was a recent divorcée whose husband took their kids back to India. She likes to shower attention on this old fool. I like having her around. She's the only bright spark in this apartment."

"Dr. Stevenson, I think we're pretty good on information from you. This will be a great help and relief to many. You may take some comfort in that," Jason said and stood up.

Willie stood up and began to turn the front door knob, "You betrayed my friendship many years ago. I don't know how to feel. I was able to help my grandmother. Maybe we'll talk about this over a drink some day."

Dr. Stevenson looked at Willie and nodded his head.

Jason and Willie closed the door behind them.

Chapter 13

"The whole episode has just brought up bad memories."

The next day Willie and Jason walked around the city. They had made it to Chapel Bridge and were about half-way down its length. The wooden covered bridge was a well-known tourist site. It was painted a dark brown with a thatched roof and many of the gables contained panes of artwork from the Middle Ages. Jason stopped to look at a painting of a baby in a crib being touched by a gruesome looking grey skeleton.

"At least we get to look around a bit before we head to the airport. We will probably need to get a corroborating story from that friend of yours, Charles Mohr. He will be a great help considering his interest in obesity." Jason looked at the wooden structure of the bridge and commented, "You know this bridge was built in the 1300s."

Willie went to one of the railings and looked out at the River Reuss.

"Hey, Stevenson did consider you a friend at one point. Before he even met Irving or Alvin Huberty," Jason said, trying to comfort him.

"It's not that. The whole episode has just brought up bad memories," Willie said while still looking at the reflection of the bridge and himself on the river's surface.

"Is it about your grandmother? I know I've asked so many times before but you know it may be helpful to let somebody know. To let your concerns see the light of day may be therapeutic," Jason offered and approached the railing that Willie was leaning against.

"So yeah, she had the experimental heart operation that Mr. Huberty said they would cover, and believe it or not they did," Willie slowly answered.

"But it didn't really work out?" Jason asked cautiously.

"There were complications. She was having a tough time breathing. It was so hard seeing her so powerless. Even when she was all swollen up, she was a strong figure. I came every day to see her," Willie said as tears began to well in his eyes.

"Did you ever speak to her again?" Jason asked.

"There was one day that they got her off the ventilator. She had a tough time talking, as she'd been attached to the machine for a whole two weeks. She told me in a raspy voice, 'Don't give up your dreams for me, my dear William.' They put her back on the ventilator the next day. The weeks turned into months with her on the ventilator. She was transferred to a long-term care facility. In the meantime, the project ended and there was no money to pay the bills. I diverted the student loan money for my college housing and tuition into my own savings account that I swore to myself I would pay later. I used that money to pay for my grandmother's care. She passed away seven months after the surgery. The college did not want me to come back after I'd used student loan money for personal use and then the bank came after me. I declared bankruptcy," Willie explained. A tear rolled down his cheek.

"It affected you profoundly," Jason stated as if he were a trained psychologist.

"I was depressed for many years. I did odd jobs to get by. I had fallen from a pretty high point in my life. I had a nice car, a nice job, a bright future. The support for that life which my grandmother and even Dr. Stevenson provided just disappeared. I was finally able to get it together enough to open that news-stand. It stands right where my folks used to have their florist shop," Willie said.

"Willie, you seem to take at least a small interest in your run-down neighborhood. You've taken a chance in building a business there when everyone else, even the bar owner next door, has deserted. That is a positive thing, a good thing that your grandmother would be very proud of," Jason offered and put his hand on Willie's back.

"I guess," Willie sighed. It was a small comfort for a man who had let time pass him by because of his sadness.

They looked out at the town of Lucerne from the bridge as the sun reached its noontime position. The town with its colorful stucco buildings looked peaceful in the distance. The mountains provided an awe inspiring backdrop. The waters of the river were very calm.

Chapter 14

"You need to quell some of this information before it gets out."

"What the fuck did you tell him?" Tony yelled at Dr. Stevenson. He lifted Dr. Stevenson with his hands and bounced Stevenson against the wall using his belly.

"Easy, easy. We can't get any information from him if you break his jaw," Elijah said.

Dr. Stevenson smelled the musk on the dirty shirt Tony had been wearing for several days. He could hear Elijah but couldn't see him behind Tony's bulky girth. "What do you want to know?" he asked.

"What did you tell the two guys that came in here? Huh," Tony screamed in his ear.

"You must have been sent by Mr. Gordon Irving," Dr. Stevenson said meekly.

"We have United States government interests," Elijah growled from his hidden position behind Tony. "Please just tell us what you passed on to the journalists."

"Only one was a journalist. Jason something-or-other. At any rate, we talked about some experiments that I did in the seventies," Dr. Stevenson offered and repeated the story he had told Jason and Willie without mentioning Gordon Irving's name. He noticed Tony's fists loosen and the grimace on his face soften.

"That's all we needed to know, thank you," Elijah said. He clicked the stop button on his tape recorder. "Tony let's wrap this up."

"Hey, I have friends in high places that keep an eye on me. If you do anything to me, Mr. Irving will be found out. So you just leave," he snapped in a panic, waiting for a pistol to be taken out.

Tony smacked him on the back of the head like a father to a son. "Ain't you cute. We don't want to kill you. Do we?"

The agents walked out the door. Dr. Stevenson wondered what mishaps may befall his friend and the journalist with him. He wiped the sweat from his brow. He had made a promise to Mr. Irving that he would not tell a soul. He thought he could just ball his guilt up inside, but somehow it had caught up with him. He also knew that Irving was a very powerful man. Stevenson kept contact with friends that could expose Irving's involvement in the obesity experiments if he were to experience an untimely demise. It was an accidental death trigger. A trigger that he thought Alvin Huberty had. Huberty had been T-boned in an intersection--ironically by an AG-World cargo van. The van had run a red light and Huberty's car burst into flames. Investigators at the scene found Huberty and the van's driver, an AG-World employee, dead. Other than the traffic violation they found nothing suspicious about the deaths. Stevenson knew other reporters like Jason Leiberman were sniffing around Huberty for a story about Gordon Irving. Huberty was more available than himself for that story. Stevenson wondered if Huberty's accidental death source was Jason Lieberman. He wondered how Jason found him when so many others had not. He knew that Willie and Jason did not have the safety triggers for "accidental death," caused possibly by the two thugs that just saw him, and he felt a little guilty. He had grown accustomed to his security of his hermitage and decided to let chance decide their fate.

Elijah flipped open his cell phone and began talking to Goldberg as soon as he left Dr. Stevenson's apartment. "Mr. Goldberg, he told us about some scheme by the company formerly known as AG-USA designed to make people gain weight. He mentioned something about a Gordon Irving. Did he mean the potential vice-presidential nominee?" Elijah asked, seeking to find out the stakes of their investigation.

Goldberg started squawking on the other line, "You *know* what you are supposed to know, now play me the tape."

Elijah used a special adapter to hook his tape recorder into his cell phone. The half-hour taped conversation went through the line and Elijah stopped it when he heard it end in his earpiece. "Did you get that?" he asked.

"Yeah I got that. This is very important. You need to quell some of this information before it gets out. It doesn't matter how fantastical or how benign Dr. Stevenson's comments sounded. You and your partner need to take care of the journalist. It is a matter of national security," Goldberg said.

"What about Dr. Stevenson himself?" Elijah asked. Elijah knew by the tone of Goldberg's voice that "take care of" meant silencing Jason Lieberman permanently. He hoped no one needed to be "taken care of" but anticipated the early demise of others.

"Stevenson has credibility problems. When he left AG-USA, they said he left due to paranoid schizophrenia. Journalist have been sniffing this story before and either they couldn't find Stevenson or they didn't bother due to his mental state," Goldberg explained on the phone.

"What about Willie Barnes?" Elijah asked.

"Barnes is a nobody. Anything he says to another random journalist would be gibberish to them. AG-USA expunged any trace of his employment anyway. Jason Lieberman, however, has a credible voice and can put multiple pieces of this puzzle together. He only needs a few more pieces of the puzzle and then he could be causing problems," Goldberg answered.

"Problems for who? Mr. Irving?" Elijah continued to interrogate his boss, as he and Tony had to carry out the task of being Grim Reaper.

"I'll figure out for who. As I said before this is a matter of national security," Goldberg stated firmly.

"I don't know if we should be doing this," Elijah said. Elijah thought about the Constitution and the fact that forth estate was used to keep the government in check. He also knew he was on a mission for his country--however absurd-- and completion of the mission would earn him a handsome bonus. The money from this mission was enough to allow him to retire early and comfortably, after just a few years more at the Secret Service.

"You were not hired to think. I told you I would get you out of the shit office you were in and into presidential detail. When I said this is national security, it means we do not give conspiracists the upper hand. The point is to make people believe in our country. Okay. I know you'll help us out. Do I need to speak to Tony?" Goldberg asked in order to right Elijah's mind.

"No." Elijah said confidently as he did not want this mission to go sloppily in his incompetent partner Tony's hands. That possibility could be harmful for himself *and* Jason Lieberman.

"Then give him my regards." Goldberg hung up the phone.

"What'd he say? Do we need to *cleanse* the area here?" Tony said.

"We need to *take care* of business in Philadelphia," Elijah corrected.

"Finally, enough of this stupid European shit. Everything's too small here. Great, Philly, finally a place to get a good meal," Tony said gleefully.

They got into the Peugeot and headed for the airport in Zurich.

Chapter 15

"You can take the feet. You'll get less messy."

"Honey, I'm going to get some coffee," Jason called to his fiancée and left their two-story row house. His neighborhood in Philadelphia was what realtors called "up and coming." This meant the impoverished were being forced out slowly by young professionals. The neighborhood still had remnants of its darker days with numerous homes that were still burnt out shells. The morning was relatively warm and that usually brought out the neighborhood kids. Jason walked down the narrow street to the local coffee shop. At the shop he bought a regular coffee for himself and a latte for his fiancée. He tucked a Sunday paper under his right arm and left the store.

He needed the walk to clear his head and start working on his book. He was also trying to clear his head from thoughts of wedding preparations. The smell of his French roast woke him up a little more. About a block ahead he could see two men coming toward him. One was a tall, thin African-American with glasses who looked very well put together in his grey suit and white shirt. The other was a white man whose belly was hanging below his belt buckle. He was wearing a brown suit but he looked significantly disheveled. Jason thought they looked like an odd couple but he was used to seeing odd couples in Philadelphia.

He made a right turn before they reached him. They turned but on the opposite side of the street.

Jason had thought that they might be heading to church but there was no church in this direction. He made a right turn and they seemed to be waiting for him.

"Hey buddy, how are you doing?" Tony asked.

Jason glanced at them, grinned and nodded his head. He didn't know them and didn't oblige them with a conversation.

"Hey I was talking to you," Tony said, less amicably.

"Huh?" Jason replied, a little stunned.

Elijah put the back of his hand on Tony's belly to keep him from teeing off.

"Mr. Jason Lieberman, correct?" Elijah asked.

"Yes, who wants to know?" Jason asked. Jason started to realize his book may be consequential to someone of import. The hair on the back of head stood on end. Whoever they were, he was a journalist and had no obligation to talk about his story.

"My name is Elijah and this is Tony. We just want to know a little bit about your fact-finding trip to Lucerne," Elijah said calmly.

"Why? Who the hell are you?" Jason asked indignantly. Thoughts ran quickly through his mind. *Who are these guys? Publishing spies? How did they know about the trip? Are they government agents?*

"Mmm latte," Tony said as he took a drink from the coffee in the paper holder Jason carried.

Jason sensed that these guys were after something more than a story. Looking at Tony, who took measured sips from his wife's coffee, he saw a sinister character that would most likely want to do more than just talk. Jason dropped his paper and his coffee and ran.

"Aw, fuck, he's gonna run," Tony said disappointed.

Jason looked around for somewhere to hide. He was only a couple of blocks from his house. He looked around to see if there were any kids or anyone out that he could call to for help. He wanted eyewitnesses for protection. He didn't know if these guys just wanted information but he'd seen the edge of a gun holster in Tony's jacket. *If it was official business, they would have shown ID right?*

He could hear someone's steps not far from him heading toward his house on the main street. The fat agent was quicker than he looked and was blocking the way to his house. He decided to go down an alley opposite his house and then turn around using a few other alleys to get to the back of his house. *Why didn't I stay at my Maryland house today?* The thin man was behind him and he knew he could outrun him to get to the back door of his house.

A hand grabbed him as he passed a burnt out home and pulled him into it. While he was running around, he realized that he couldn't hear what direction the footsteps were coming or going. Jason looked straight into the fat agent's eyes. His angry grimace was framed by a stubbly beard and sweaty forehead. Jason couldn't speak.

Whifft.

Tony left the shell of a building and found Elijah doubled over trying to catch his breath.

"It's taken care of. Bring the car over and we can load the body in. You know you're really gonna have to get in shape for Presidential duty," Tony said very calmly.

Elijah went to get the car while Tony kept an eye on Jason's body. Tony took the silencer off of his pistol and put the gun back in his holster. A moment later the black Mercury drove down the alley. Elijah got out of the car.

"You can take the feet. You'll get less messy," Tony said.

Elijah was not used to seeing dead bodies and just nodded his head. They picked up Jason's body and threw it into the trunk of the Mercury. Elijah and Tony got into the car and drove out of the alley.

"There's a place in the Schuylkill River swamps we can dump him. You know I learned a little something from working on mob cases," Tony said with a smile on his face.

Elijah grunted and loosened his collar. A lump grew in his throat from his guilt.

"At least now maybe we can get back to the crime fighting we are supposed to be doing," Tony quipped with some relief and a bit of sarcasm.

Chapter 16

"Neptune, I hope you finish Jason's story."

"Newspaper man, where have you been?" yelled a neighborhood kid to Willie. He was wearing a grey pullover and a gold cross on a chain.

"I didn't know you kids cared. What do you want: a candy bar, potato chips, a carrot?" Willie asked with a new perspective on weight.

"Just asking man, no need to get so defensive. We all thought you moved out to where the customers lived," the kid smirked, implying he had moved his newsstand to a white neighborhood. He was unfazed by the "carrot" non-sequitur.

Willie was surprised to hear a hint of acknowledgement from "the store"-- that is, the drug dealers' corner; the only other business on the block. He didn't think that they even knew he existed. He tested the child: "hey--I dare you to read this."

The kid grabbed the *New York Times* from Willie's outstretched hands and started reading out loud. He was twelve years old and stumbled over some of the words. Willie listened and corrected pronunciation when it was needed. He also added definitions where he thought necessary. While he listened, Willie straightened up the stand and took inventory. Suddenly though, the stream of words stopped.

"Yo, Willie, ain't this your friend?" the kid asked, pointing at a picture on the page. The boy remembered the strange, small, white man that had come to see Willie and how the kids had tossed him back and forth before Willie broke it up.

"Keep reading," Willie replied from underneath the counter.

"Writer Jason Lip, Lieb…" the kid had trouble getting around Jason's last name.

"What? That's Lieberman," Willie said, still busying himself with news-stand chores.

"Yeah, that's right," the kid replied and nodded. He continued: "Writer Jason Lieberman found shot dead in Philadelphia."

"What?" Willie shouted. He immediately stood up and grabbed the paper from the kid. The paper showed Jason's last book picture. Willie's shoulders shrunk. He felt defeated. *Who could do this? What a waste. I brought up those ugly memories for what? The bad guys always win.* He had a hunch that it wasn't a random Philadelphia shooting. Jason was working on a conspiracy of a very important man who had too much to lose.

"Sorry 'bout your friend. I gotta go," the kid offered and walked off to "the store."

Willie just stared at the paper. The words seemed to flow together as if the ink was still wet and the paper was glass. *What do I do now?* He debated if he should just go on like he had never met Jason. He could stay isolated like Dr. Stevenson. He remembered his grandmother again and the pain of her loss. He also remembered the regret on the bridge in Lucerne and what hiding away had cost him.

Willie grabbed the metal gate of the newsstand and locked up. It gave its usual squeal. He locked the padlock and walked to his faithful steed, the Lincoln. It took a couple of turns of the ignition but eventually started. He drove toward the North entrance of I-95. Philadelphia was only a couple hours away. He needed to find Jason's notes. He needed to get the story out. Jason's story would not die and neither would his own.

$$* \quad * \quad *$$

Jason's brick row home was painted a dark red and had white trim around the windows and doors. The door itself was also white. There were kids playing in the street. One boy was sitting on the handlebars of a bicycle a girl was peddling. Willie had pulled over to look at the house and cracked his door open a little. The street smelled of garbage. Bins were out for the collection but they hadn't been picked up yet, even though it was three in the afternoon. Willie drove around the block a few times to find a parking spot large enough for the Lincoln.

He got out of the car a block and a half away from Jason's house. He hoped someone was there. People had to know about the additive and their future Vice President. Willie knocked on the door softly. No one answered. He knocked again with a bit more force. The door opened.

"Yes?" a man in his fifties asked in a gruff, stern voice. His eyebrows were thick and he had a distinct, almost permanent-looking frown. He wore a red plaid shirt and white khaki pants. The man only opened the door about eight inches so he could easily close it.

"Hi, uh, my name is Willie Barnes. I was an associate of Jason's," Willie started with some trepidation. He hadn't expected a man like this, probably Jason's father, to be answering the door.

"Yeah and so, you know what happened," the man said in an aggravated and suspicious tone.

"I was wondering if I could talk about Jason's book," Willie said and swallowed.

"Well, do you know what happened? We don't want to talk to anyone. We're grieving. We don't care about the publishing right now, okay? Get lost. No, go tell your bosses…" the man trailed off. The ridges in his brow got larger. His voice got louder.

"But it's important——" Willie was beginning to see that his trip here was futile.

"Wait," whispered a female voice in the background, behind the door.

"Hold on," the man sighed and left the door open about an inch.

Willie waited outside for what seemed like twenty minutes. He could hear bickering going on inside. Finally the door opened completely. The man with the frown still chiseled into his face waved for him to enter and Willie walked into the home. In front of him stood a very thin, fair-skinned woman with dark black hair that was tied back. She looked like she had been crying continuously. Her eyes were bloodshot and there were dark rings around them. She was wringing her hands in the white sweatshirt she was wearing.

"Thank you for coming, Mr. Barnes. My name is Lucy. I am--was--Jason's fiancée," she whispered. She knew exactly who he was, though she'd never met him. She looked straight into his eyes as she spoke.

"He spoke a lot about you on our trip to Switzerland," Willie said with an apologetic grin.

"Please come in," she offered and ushered him into the living room. The room was a yellow color. A large window faced the street. Orange drapery hung alongside the window. The room seemed unusually cheerful. She motioned for Willie to have a seat on what looked like put-together furniture from Ikea. The man who had answered the door was keeping a watchful eye on Willie but after they moved into the living room he walked upstairs to the second floor.

"I'm sorry for your loss. I wanted to know if I could still talk to you about Jason's work during this trying time," Willie said. He didn't want to delve too deeply into the cause of Jason's death. He thought if he talked about his life it would be easier. He remembered this from his own painful bereavement. Willie smelled the flowers from several bouquets that were in the house.

"Mr. Barnes, I can't talk about him right now. But I will give you his notes," Lucy said solemnly. They had been seated only a few minutes when she went to retrieve Jason's notebook.

Willie looked out the window while he waited for her. The garbage men had finally come to collect the trash. He then looked to his right at the fireplace and the photos on the mantle of Lucy and Jason on vacation trips. Willie thought of the mantel in his own home where there were picture-perfect images of relationships, like his parents and grandmother that had ended too soon. At least for now, he shared with Lucy the emptiness that beautiful images like these could not fill. She was young and thin with long, brown hair and high cheek bones. He knew she wouldn't be alone for long. Lucy walked in with a leather-bound notebook with notes sticking out of the sides. She handed it to Willie without saying anything and sat back on the couch.

"Thank you again for coming. I'm glad you want to see his notes," she said softly.

"I need to get this information out. Jason would want that," Willie replied. He looked through the book. Little notes fell to the ground as he turned the pages. They were the little ideas that he had written down on scraps of paper when he hadn't had the entire notebook with him. The pages seemed to be covered in haphazard writing in different colored pen. Some of the text was highlighted. Dr. Stevenson's story was written just the way Stevenson had recounted it. A few pages before that was the chemical formula and analysis of the additive that Willie found in the old box truck. Willie was pleased he didn't find the account of his grandmother's death or her stay in the intensive care unit.

"Mr. Barnes, when Jason spoke of you, he said you were a man of great courage," she offered and made a great effort to give a small smile.

Willie looked up from the notebook at the smile. "Please, call me Willie, or if you prefer, Neptune," he said and smiled back. He wondered how he could get the story out. He wondered if Jason's timing of the election was off or was he a very fast writer, as the convention was in only a month's time. By publishing time, Gordon Irving could already be in office. Willie knew he wasn't a writer and was not going get the book done in time. *Maybe I could get his information to another reporter. No one will believe me. I need another witness or someone who understands what we did in that lab.* He turned a few more pages and found a card for Dr. Charles Mohr's weight management clinic. Dr. Mohr was a reliable source. He needed to know there was something more to the obesity epidemic. He specialized in the disease. Willie closed the book.

"Why Neptune?" Lucy asked.

Willie stood up with the notebook. "I was an all-American high school swimmer. It's been a long time since this champ has heard his nickname," Willie grinned and shook his head, as if it was only in his imagination.

"Neptune, I hope you finish Jason's story," she said, searching for hope in Willie's eyes.

"Jason wanted to reveal the truth about how our government helped engineer the obesity epidemic. I'm not a writer but I will find some old friends who can help me with this. We'll get the story out," he promised, looking into her eyes. He rubbed her shoulder with his right hand and then walked toward the front door. Lucy followed him. He heard the shuffle of her slippers behind him. He paused and she opened the door for him. He hugged her without saying a word.

"Thanks," she whispered as Willie walked out onto the stoop.

Willie turned to see her leaning on the door jamb with tears running down her face. The old man who had answered the door had come downstairs and grabbed her by the shoulders. He brought her into the house.

It was already late and the children who had been playing on the block had all gone inside. On the far end of the block he saw a cluster of kids minding a "store" just like the one by his newsstand. He decided that he was too tired to make the three hour trek back to D.C. and climbed into the old Lincoln. He drove around thinking about staying in a motel but ended up parking his car on a lot by a construction site between the University of Pennsylvania and Drexel University. He climbed into the back seat. The rumble of busses passing by him was like the crashing of waves as he drifted off to sleep. He dreamt about Charles Mohr's willingness to join him and getting the story out as he had told Lucy he would do.

Chapter 17

"You and I, look at us--we would be dead in caveman days."

I t was eleven o'clock in the morning and Willie had pulled into the parking lot of the weight management center. The clinic was a one-story building with Spanish villa features. It had a dark brown tile roof and burnt orange stucco walls. There was a small porch with a few plants. There were several arches that bordered the roof of the building. A large, dark wooden door was used for the entryway. It was a comforting structure that did not say "you must do this," but "let us meet your needs."

Willie got out of his car and walked along the path toward the front door. He paused at the staircase by a yellow rose bush. He felt apprehensive and wondered if too much time had passed. Young Charlie Mohr was probably a different character than Dr. Charles Mohr. *What the hell am I thinking? He doesn't owe me anything. He'll probably think that I want something, like I'm some kind of bum. He doesn't owe Jason anything. Hell, he has made a ton of money off of people being fat.* Willie started to turn back to the Lincoln. "Ahh," he sighed in frustration and faced the clinic door again. *That's not life, this is.* He reached for the doorknob and entered the waiting area.

It was a large waiting area. Pleasant, nondescript music came from two small speakers in the corners of the room. The smell of cinnamon filled the air. A brown leather bench seat curled around three walls. There were no patients in any of the chairs. Shade-tolerant plants sat in the window sills. In the center of the waiting area was a small, round coffee table with magazines scattered on its surface. The fourth wall had a small window for the receptionist. Willie walked up to this window.

"Can I help you?" the receptionist asked, sounding a bit startled.

Willie remembered that he had just spent the night in the back seat of his car. He had a slight gristle on his cheeks. His soft, brown leather jacket was wrinkled. He was hoping he didn't smell too bad. He also stood out as he was a relatively thin man in a weight management clinic. "Uh, yes. I know I don't have an appointment, but could you let Dr. Mohr know that an old friend, Willie Barnes, wanted to talk to him?" Willie implored with a tremble in his voice.

"Let me see if he can see you. Have a seat," the receptionist replied. She nodded her head as she walked back to the clinical offices.

"Actually, can I use you restroom?" Willie asked, still with a wavering voice.

The receptionist stopped on her way to the offices and turned around with an annoyed expression on her face. "It's on your right," she motioned.

Willie opened the door and went inside. He looked at himself and thought about what a mess he was. He washed his face two or three times with cold water. He took about ten disposable towels to wipe his face. He opened the door.

A lanky man in a grey suit was standing by the receptionist station. He was wearing reading glasses and looking at a medical journal. He looked up, closed the journal and smiled. "Willie Neptune Barnes! It's been a good, long while," Dr. Mohr proclaimed. He stuck out his hand.

Willie reached out his hand. Charles pulled him toward him for a hug. "Hey, hey, Charlie Mohr. How have you been?"

"You know, I thought this guy was the coolest man on the planet when I was a kid," Charles said to the receptionist as he pointed to Willie. "So what's up?" he asked Willie.

"Well, I wanted to talk—" Willie started to say.

"Ah. It's almost lunch. Do you have plans? Let's go to the deli around the corner. They have some tables outside. It's relatively warm today," Charles interrupted. He was so excited about seeing a friend from the past. The sight of Willie in his brown leather jacket had suddenly given him an injection of youthful vitality.

They walked to the deli, making small talk. Willie talked about the drive from Philly and sleeping in his car. Charles talked about how fortunate it was to see Willie, otherwise he would have eaten his limp turkey sandwich in his office while dictating charts. Charles bought them both lunch and they sat at a metal café table that had a post for an umbrella although there wasn't one hanging from it.

"Let's not spend all lunch on catch-up. Willie, what's going on? Why did you find me?" Charles asked. He hoped it wasn't money, and a second later he felt guilty about thinking Willie had sought him out to find some cash.

"I need help regarding obesity and the causes of it," Willie began to say.

"Willie, you may have a forty-something gut, but I can't recommend any medication or surgical weight loss for you," Charles said with a confused smile on his face.

"No, no, not for me. It's about Dr. Stevenson's work and my implications in it," Willie replied, shaking his head. Willie proceeded to tell Charles about the appetite enhancer and the involvement of Gordon Irving. He also told him about Jason and his book to expose Irving's weight study. Willie stopped and sighed. He realized he had ventured into political waters and maybe Dr. Charles Mohr was a big fan of Irving.

"Willie, you are implying Irving and his company have contributed to the worldwide obesity epidemic," Charles offered skeptically. "I am unsure how much you know about weight gain, so let me give you a brief lesson about what we know now. Energy in equals energy out. So, if you eat too much and you don't burn the weight off, you are liable to get heavy. There are certain controls to this process that emanate from the brain and peripherally, either from fat tissue or the stomach. Genes probably determine if these hormones cause us to retain energy. As cavemen, it was important to retain energy at all costs because there just wasn't that much food around. You and I, look at us--we would be dead in caveman days. It's the advent of agriculture that has kept our gene pool around," Charles said emphatically and took a sip of his iced tea.

"Jason told me that the increase in carbohydrates in our diets correlated with weight gain. I put the additive that Dr. Stevenson was working on *in carbohydrates*," Willie emphatically replied.

"Willie, there are just more carbohydrates around. A lot of things have changed; schools don't have gym class any more, and almost all kids' TV is dominated by food advertising," Charles explained.

"How do you know that Dr. Stevenson's research start the avalanche that is obesity?" Willie asked.

"The picture's too complicated. Tell your friend, Jason, he's really reaching here," Charles insisted, a cynical smile on his face. It seemed like a ridiculous theory to him.

"I'd love to. He's dead," Willie said coldly.

"Oh, I'm sorry, what happened?" Charles asked, wondering how the author had died.

"They found him in a swamp in Philadelphia. They don't think it was a robbery," Willie said.

"That's weird," Charles answered, hoping that Willie would talk about something else.

"I'm beginning to think that somebody thinks they got caught with their hand in the cookie jar."

"What?" Charles didn't get the analogy.

"I think somebody doesn't want the general public to know about the studies that Mr. Irving commissioned," Willie said firmly.

"So you think a friend of Gordon Irving killed this author?"

"Yes. Think about it: Dr. Stevenson lives in isolation in Switzerland. Jason gets all the pieces of the puzzle and now he's dead in a swamp."

"What about you? Are you next?" Charles asked, wondering if Willie believed he was next on Irving's hit list. He didn't believe the conspiracy theory and thought it was just ridiculous. He didn't know Jason but he could have been killed for a variety of reasons.

"I'm not worth getting rid of. Look at me. I'm an old, depressed newsstand guy with no biology degree spouting off about a conspiracy. I should be committed. That's why I came to you. I have Jason's notes. You know, come to think of it, with your intimate knowledge of clinical obesity and the research at Stevenson's lab, someone should be keeping an eye on you," Willie pointed out.

"I don't know about *that*," Charles said doubtfully.

"I'm surprised. You had intimate knowledge of the additives when you were a kid and now you are a weight management guy. I'm surprised you never got jumped by Mr. Irving's henchmen or somebody from AGWorld" Willie said.

"From what?" Charles asked.

"AGWorld, of course," Willie clarified.

Charles stared off into space, zoning out from the conversation. He needed to make a phone call.

"I think it would be important for everyone to know who their new vice president is and what he's done," Willie said.

Charles kept staring off into the distance.

"So, can you help me get this story out?" Willie asked.

"Willie, can I get your number? I have to think about this. This is a pretty hefty accusation. You can't just smear somebody that big without facts. I just need to think about it," Charles said hurriedly.

"Please do. Look over these notes. I copied them from Jason's notebook." Willie handed him a stack of photocopies.

"Good to see you again, Willie," Charles said and grinned.

Willie stood up and patted Charles on the back. He walked out of the deli and back toward the Lincoln in the weight clinic's parking lot.

Charles sat in the deli for a few more minutes. He sighed, stood up, and went back to the clinic to finish seeing his afternoon patients.

Willie sat behind the faded wheel of his Lincoln and looked out at the weight clinic. He knew he had done all he could to get the message out. But right now he felt like a student again--one that had completed his exam on a Friday, but would have to wait all weekend to get his grade.

Chapter 18

"Thanks for being honest with me."

Charles sat down in the leather swivel chair behind the large wooden desk in his home office. He had been dwelling on Willie's conspiracy theory throughout the day. *Maybe this has something to do with that FBI agent?* He had tucked in his daughter and kissed his wife goodnight. Rummaging through the bottom drawer of the desk, he dug Daria's phone number out. He knew exactly where it was. It was on a small scrap from the corner of a drug company pad. He laid it on the table and debated calling her, fidgeting with his cell phone, picking it up and putting it down.

What if she changed her number? What am I going to ask her? Am I really doing this because I believe Willie's story? Do I want to know her answer? He lifted his knees up and down nervously and pushed the scrap paper and his phone to the side.

He bent down and picked up the notes that Willie gave him, which were lying by his feet. The theory seemed outlandish to him. *One man could not be responsible for the obesity epidemic. A scientist at least could not or should not believe this idea.* He buried himself in Jason's notes. He saw the data that he worked on as a teen in Dr. Stevenson's lab. He didn't know how the journalist got this data. From what he remembered, much of the work was not published and was handwritten in lab note books. In the journalist's notes, the source of the data came from AG-USA. Serial numbers on study materials correlated with that of corporate records. He also remembered AG-USA on the boxes Willie had been moving for special project for Dr. Stevenson, many years ago. Charles took out his laptop and went to the Centers for Disease Control website. He found the page that indicated carbohydrate intake increasing over time correlated with increases in obesity in the United States. In Jason's notes, a similar graph showed AG-USA profits climbing with increases in carbohydrate intake by Americans. *It still seems to be coincidence.* He kept searching for the rise of Gordon Irving. There were photos and notes of Mr. Irving's interactions with good friends in the FDA and congress in the 1970s. Jason had also noted how many bills happened to favor AG-USA. Charles saw how some of the people directly involved with the additive project were pushed aside. Dr. Stevenson left with profound guilt and found a hermitage in Switzerland. Willie suffered deep depression and kept himself hidden in the inner city of D.C. Alan Huberty, who had become the chief financial officer of the new AGWorld, mysteriously died in a hit and run. Now, the author who had put all the pieces together was found in a swamp in Philadelphia on his way to get coffee. He remembered his own strange encounter with Michael Goldberg. *Maybe, it was him.* He couldn't prove it. His pulse began to increase.

Charles looked at the family picture with himself and Heather behind their daughter. He felt a heightened threat to his own safety. He picked up his cell phone and dialed the number on the paper.

"Daria?" Charles whispered.

"What? Hang on a minute," Daria said on the line. In the background, was the thumping bass of a dance club. "Yes, who is it?" she asked.

"It's me, Charles," he said cautiously.

"Oh," Daria said with sad surprise.

"Don't hang up. I need to ask you something."

"Come on. I'm just trying to get over you. I don't want to meet you out anywhere. I'm in Miami with some friends. I—" she started to raise her voice.

Charles sensed that she might hang up on him. "Wait, no. I need your help please. It's not about us. I mean it is but what I'm trying to find out is why you chose me," Charles began.

"Oh." Daria calmed down but sounded disappointed.

The dance club music seemed to fade away as if she had left the club to hear what had to say.

"This may sound ridiculous, but did AGWorld want you to find out information about me?" Charles asked cautiously.

"I quit one month ago. I don't know, maybe. No," Daria answered with trepidation.

"Please. What do you mean *maybe*? It's important," Charles said, more commandingly.

"Okay. You remember Sheldon Hairston? The guy you met in Denver a long time ago? I had to tell him," she said.

"Tell him what?" Charles asked with anticipation.

"I had to tell him of your obesity theories and about any connections you found with corporations, more specifically, AGWorld and obesity."

"What did you tell him?"

"I don't know. There wasn't much to tell. He didn't seem to react to anything I said."

"Why did you do it?"

"I owed them for my education and wanted to clear my loans. They paid for everything and I could shorten my time with the company. I hated that stupid company. I didn't mean to hurt you. I loved you. It seemed harmless enough," Daria's voice softened.

"What did you tell them when we broke it off?" Charles asked, thinking there may be some retribution.

"I told them I couldn't care less about the information I was getting on you and after a couple of months gave in my resignation. I just wanted you, that's all," Daria said.

"Unfortunately, we know that can't happen. Thanks for being honest with me. Best of luck in whatever you decide to do. Have a good time wherever you are," Charles said soothingly but curtly. He didn't want his heart to run away as it did when they had first met. He hung up the phone.

"Wait Charles, I—" Daria tried to fit in a few words before he hung up. She knew that was the last she would hear from him.

Charles turned off his phone and went upstairs. He tried to get to sleep. Tossing and turning, he thought about how he would need to get a hold of Willie. *I was part of the list of people who knew.* There was a writer with the *Washington News* he knew. First thing in the morning could not come soon enough. They would let the whole world know about how one man had helped changed the health of a nation. *That man couldn't be the number two man of the most powerful country in the world--and maybe even president someday.* He felt good, scared, and at the same time, youthfully energetic. He looked at Heather sleeping peacefully next to him and tried to calm down. Somehow he managed to get in three hours of sleep before morning.

Chapter 19

"Never too early for Jack Daniel's and diet Dr. Pepper."

One week later after his realization, Dr. Charles Mohr woke up early to get to Washington. He had discussed at length with his reporter friend at the *Washington News* about Jason's notes and his own personal experience of being watched. His friend at the *News* had told him last night the Jason's notes would be made into a feature article and that story was ready for publication. The reporter told him that this was going to be a historic revelation about the potential vice presidential candidate. Charles was going to drive to Washington to be with Willie who was the source of most of the information. The two had spoken consistently for the past week, talking about the additive and the good old days in Stevenson's lab. A lot of burden on Willie's shoulders seemed to have lifted and Charles wondered if it was the same feeling he had when he let Daria go. He sped down I-95 with a sense of purpose, ducking and weaving through traffic. Willie had told him that the *News* got delivered to his stand at five.

He was finally in Washington. He hated D.C. because of the circular streets. He could never find his way around town. He finally found the street that Willie's stand was on and parked in front of it. Willie wasn't there yet. Charles looked at the tiny newsstand structure that didn't appear to go too far deep. He was a little wary of the neighborhood with its burnt-out buildings. He didn't know whether to feel comforted or afraid of the lack of people around. The dilapidated bar next door looked like the place Willie had described to the *News* journalist. Next to the bar looked like a stack of papers that must have just been delivered. Dr. Mohr got out of his car to take a look.

As he got closer, he wondered if he should take a look at them immediately or wait until Willie opened his stand. The bundle was strapped tight with a plastic band and the front page was covered with an advertisement. Dr. Mohr was a bit disappointed and took a seat on top of the papers. He wondered if their story would have any effect on obesity. *Would the food industry see its role in the disease? Would the government put greater restrictions on food additives? Would people with obesity find any solace in knowing that corporations had a hand in their weight gain?*

The sun started to peek over the rooftops of the row homes. The shadows of chimneys and TV antennae looked like people welcoming the sun. Headlights came toward the newsstand. It was Willie's Lincoln. Willie parked behind Charles' car, got out and walked toward the physician.

"I'm surprised to see you this morning. You know a fancy doctor wandering this neck of the woods at this time of day is not a good idea. It's not good for your health," Willie said with a smile. He knew the story was due to be published but didn't know the exact day. He also didn't think Charles would come to his newsstand. He felt glad to see him though.

Charles stood up to greet Willie. "I wanted to see what kind of an impact the coolest guy I know made on the world today," Charles said with the same admiration of his teen years. He shook Willie's hand.

"Have you seen the story yet?" Willie asked.

"No. I thought we could look at together. Plus, I couldn't get through the binding that they have on the bales," Charles said.

Willie laughed at his answer. He bent down to undo the metal gate of his newsstand. He grunted when he lifted the door. Making his way behind the counter of the stand, he grabbed a utility knife and waved Charles away from the bales.

"Well, let's see what we got," Willie said. He slashed away the plastic strap and removed a paper.

Charles bent down to take a look. Willie removed the advertising section. The bale contained *The Washington News* but their story was not the lead head-line. However, there was an image of Gordon Irving being led away in handcuffs on the upper half of the paper.

"Willie, turn it over," Charles said.

Willie picked up the paper and looked at it closely. He then flipped it over. "What the hell?"

Charles read the caption below the photo:

"Agriculture Secretary and Potential Vice Presidential nominee Gordon Irving charged with insider trading and illegal transfer of funds from AGWorld to pharmaceutical com-pany, arrested early this morning. Behind him is his assistant, Marc Olesson, who gave information to the Securities and Exchange Commission."

Willie found their story in the right hand corner. Only one paragraph of the story had made it onto the front page. "There it is," Willie said and read the title: "Gordon Irving and Obesity: Profits Killing Americans."

Charles read it very quickly and turned to the remainder of the story inside the paper. Willie did it more slowly, disappointed that their story wasn't the headline. Their story *did* take up a whole page in the paper.

"It's all there," Charles said.

"Yeah," Willie put down the paper and started to move the other bunches of papers into his stand.

"We can't say for sure what kind of impact this will have. Willie, you can't be so disappointed. You did good. We did good. We've revealed this cover up that has been going on for years. It's up to the readers to feel outraged and maybe this one story will turn things around," Charles said. He helped Willie bring some papers into the stand.

Willie watched as Charles awkwardly carried the bale of papers wearing his suit jacket. "What the hell are you doing?" he asked.

"Helping," Charles tossed the bundles on the stand's floor.

"Do you think we'll make any difference?" Willie asked. He looked at Charles, who looked exhausted after carrying a few loads of papers.

"Willie, I think we did what we could. We aren't Greek gods, although we may be nicknamed for them. And we aren't going to carry the burden of obesity on our backs any more. It's a greater problem than Gordon Irving. We can let it go. I think what you did made Jason, and most definitely your grandmother, proud."

"Hmmh," Willie half-smiled.

"Willie, you're still a young guy. I looked up to you when I was a kid. I thought you could do anything. I believe you still can. We've done our part. Let's see what the future holds. Let's see if our story gets people to think about our leaders and about who is feeding us."

"Okay. Fine," Willie began to cave in. "I guess this whole trip was a little bit of an eye-opener for me. I know I've got to get back on track. Thanks for the spiel. I appreciate it. But before we say goodbye to the past let's send it off with a toast," Willie said with a smile on his face. He ducked under the counter and pulled out a full bottle of Jack Daniel's and soda. "Been saving this for a special occasion," Willie said.

"Isn't it too early for a drink?" Charles asked with a puzzled expression on his face.

"Never too early for Jack Daniel's and *diet* Dr. Pepper," Willie said with a smile and began to pour the mixture together in two glasses. He handed one glass to Charles and took hold of his own.

They clinked their glasses and downed their drinks in celebration.